SILKE JUSTICE

by

KEN FARMER

Cover Art by Rush Cole
rushcolefineart@aol.com
www.rushcolefineart.com

AUTHOR

Ken Farmer didn't write his first full novel until he was sixty-nine years of age. He often wonders what the hell took him so long. At age seventy-seven...he's currently working on novel number twenty-seven.

Ken spent thirty years raising cattle and quarter horses in Texas and forty-five years as a professional actor (after a stint in the Marine Corps). Those years gave him a background for storytelling...or as he has been known to say, "I've always been a bit of a bull---t artist, so writing novels kind of came naturally once it occurred to me I could put my stories down on paper."

Ken's writing style has been likened to a combination of Louis L'Amour and Terry C. Johnston with an occasional Hitchcockian twist...now that's a combination.

In addition to his love for writing fiction, he likes to teach acting, voice-over and writing workshops. His favorite expression is: "Just tell the damn story."

Writing has become Ken's second life: he has been a Marine, played collegiate football, been a Texas wildcatter, cattle and horse rancher, professional film and TV actor and director, and now...a novelist. Who knew?

Ken Farmer's dialogue flows like a beautiful western river...it's the gold standard...Carole Beers

Web page: www.KenFarmer-Author.net

ISBN-13: 978-1-7329119-7-0
ISBN-10: 1-7329119-7-5

Timber Creek Press
Imprint of Timber Creek Productions, LLC
312 N. Commerce St.
Gainesville, Texas 76240

Published by: Timber Creek Press
timbercreekpresss@yahoo.com
www.timbercreekpress.net
Twitter: @pagact
Facebook Book Page:
www.facebook.com/TimberCreekPress
Ken's email: pagact@yahoo.com
214-533-4964

DEDICATION

This tome is number one in the new spin-off from the Bone & Loraine series...the SILKE JUSTICE series. I dedicate it to Rush Cole, the lovely and talented artist that is responsible for the cover. The painting is titled Peacemaker Varmint Tamer and was a perfect fit for my character of SILKE JUSTICE. Thank you, Rush.

ACKNOWLEDGMENT

The author gratefully acknowledges Lt. Colonel Clyde DeLoach, USMC (Ret.), Buck Stienke, Terry Heflin - retired English Professor at Tarrant County College, and award-winning, best-selling novelist Mary Deal, for their invaluable help in proofing, beta reading and editing this novel.

This novel is a work of fiction...except the parts that aren't. Names, characters, places, and incidents are either the products of the author's imagination or are used fictitiously. Any resemblance to actual persons, living or dead, business establishments, events, or locales is entirely coincidental, except where they aren't.

FORWARD
by Ken Farmer

Silke Justice is twenty-three years old. She's a 5'6", blue-eyed, strawberry blond who has been a detective for the Pinkerton National Detective Agency for three years.

Her full name is Silke Diane Justice...Silke is a Germanic derivative from Latin, a form of Celia...meaning 'heavenly'. Her middle name, Diane...means 'divine'.

Silke Diane Justice—Heavenly Divine Justice.

As she says, "I'm an awesome, redheaded, Southern belle, with a dash of bulldog, a splash of gator, a double measure of sass, a hell of a left hook...and I can shoot the flies off a bull's ass at fifty yards."

I introduced Silke in *Bone's Enigma* when the Big John Tackett gang raided the Justin ranch in Cooke County, Texas, and murdered her parents.

She joined up with Bone and Loraine and Bass Reeves to track down the murderers—along with a time-traveler from 2018—in the Chickasaw Nation.

They kill all but Duce Walton, who escapes.

Her adventure continues with her own series in *SILKE JUSTICE*, her black, blue-eyed, half wolf...Bear Dog, and Chickasaw Lighthorse, Red Wolf as they track Duce Walton and his new gang that are robbing trains belonging to the KATY railroad in Texas and the Nations.

They are joined by Texas Rangers, Riley Boston and Bodie Hickman, along with Bone and Loraine.

Suck your hat down and cinch up...and be prepared for a ride.

TIMBER CREEK PRESS

CHAPTER ONE

HENRIETTA, TEXAS

"Children, please turn in your readers to page twenty-two..."

Two fifteen year old freckle-faced boys, wearing faded blue bib overalls, in the back of the room, one on the left side and the other on the right, were throwing a homemade baseball back and forth.

"Boys, stop that," said the prim, attractive strawberry blond teacher at the front of the room.

The two boys ignored her and continued their game of pitch. They had taken a rubber ball and wrapped two inches of kite string tightly around it, making it a serviceable, if a bit rough, ball for their baseball game they played every afternoon.

"I'm not going to say it again, boys…"

The two ruffians continued to ignore the new, twenty-three year old substitute teacher.

Some of the other mixed grade students smirked at the two boys doing what they called, *breakin' in* the new schoolmarm.' None of them noticed the young woman open her desk drawer because they were being entertained watching the pitch and catch across the room at the back.

They all started and several of the girls screamed at the tremendous roar of a handgun discharge from the front of the room, and then as a cloud of white gunsmoke billowed out, the ball flew apart in midair like a shot quail. It fluttered to the floor and bounced twice with the string unraveling until it came to rest.

The entire class jumped to their feet and looked at the hole completely through the homemade ball, sending the string askew.

They turned around and stared at the teacher as she blew the smoke from the muzzle of her ivory-gripped .38-40 Colt Peacemaker and placed it back in her desk drawer. Everyone's eyes were big as saucers and every mouth hung open.

The two boys stood frozen in time for a long moment. They stared at the remains of their ball, looked at each other, and then slowly turned and looked at the teacher with looks of amazement compounded with awe—then fear.

"Now, if I have *everyone's* attention…please turn to page twenty-two of your McGuffey readers," said Elizabeth Longmire—undercover Pinkerton detective, Silke Justice.

As one, and without a word, the class quietly sat down and quickly opened their books.

The one room white clapboard schoolhouse stood at the edge of the Henrietta downtown only a half of a mile from the east to west railroad tracks just south of the Red River.

It was a mixed grade school, from seventh through eleventh grades in the morning and one through sixth grades in the afternoon.

A well-dressed man in his thirties boarded the westbound Wichita Falls Railway coal-fired train at the depot in Henrietta. It would join the Missouri-Kansas-Texas Railroad, known as the KATY, in Wichita Falls.

He nodded and tipped his gray Stetson at a middle-aged woman holding the hand of her six-year old daughter as he stood aside and let the pair pass to choose their seats.

"Ma'am."

"Thank you, sir," she responded.

He chose a forward facing seat at the rear of the passenger car and unfolded a copy of the *Clay County Chieftain* newspaper he had picked up in the depot.

The engineer up in the cab of the big black 4x4x2 locomotive released the tall Johnson bar, putting the four-foot tall drive wheels in gear.

They initially slipped a little and then gained purchase on the steel rails and slowly picked up speed as the locomotive chugged out of town, belching a voluminous column of black smoke from its stack.

SILKE JUSTICE

The train gained speed as it headed west toward Wichita Falls on its short eighteen mile journey across the bucolic countryside of north Texas.

Nine miles out of Henrietta, the train passed through the small community of Jolly and the rear door to the car opened as the blue-clad conductor entered from the caboose.

"Tickets! Have your tickets ready, please."

He turned to the man in the forward-facing seat for his anticipated ticket, but faced the barrel of a .45 caliber Colt Peacemaker.

The passenger got to his feet and stepped behind the frightened conductor and pressed the muzzle against the man's spine.

"Now, stay calm mister…this ain't gonna take too long…I'll have that little shooter you got in yer pocket."

"You won't git away with this, friend," said the conductor as he handed him his .32 caliber, five shot revolver.

"One, I ain't yer friend and two, this ain't my first rodeo."

"Oh! You're the gentleman bandit, ain'tcha?"

He grinned. "That what they're callin' me?"

The conductor nodded.

The robber chuckled and addressed the almost full car. "Folks, this is what's known as a holdup. Don't do anything stupid and this conductor won't get his spine shot in two...You men get out all your cash, wallets, guns an' watches, an' you ladies remove your jewelry. Gonna be passin' along the aisle with a flour sack. Put what you got in it...Wouldn't be smart to hold back, neither."

There were frightened mutterings up and down the car from the mostly business men making their daily commute to the larger city of Wichita Falls.

The bandit moved along the aisleway as the car rocked back and forth, pushing the conductor, with his hands over his head, in front of him. He held out his sack to each side of the aisle for the passengers to drop their valuables in.

One well-dressed man with a gray Homberg hat and carrying a leather valise, held it tightly to his chest.

"Open it," commanded the robber.

"No, no, please," the man protested.

The bandit swung his pistol to the man's forehead and thumbed the hammer back, making ominous clicking sounds.

The business man's head dropped as he opened the valise and took out several wrapped bundles of orange one hundred dollar gold certificate bills stamped, *Payable to Bearer.*

"Just the feller I was lookin' for," said the robber with a grin.

They reached the forward end of the car and suddenly the fiftyish conductor twisted around and attempted to grab the robber's gun. The brigand shoved the muzzle against the man's stomach and pulled the trigger.

Most of the women in the car screamed at the roar of the gunshot as the conductor cried out and collapsed to the floor like so much wet newspaper.

His blue jacket with brass buttons running the length of the garment, burst into flames around the bullet hole, but rapidly went out as blood soaked the cloth. It added the stench of burning wool to the cloud of acrid gunsmoke already filling the closed car.

"This is what stupid gets you." He glanced out the window as the train slowed coming into the outskirts of Wichita Falls.

He tipped his hat to the passengers as he opened the door at the forward end of the car. "Much obliged folks, ya'll have a nice day…Hear?"

The train had slowed to about five miles an hour as it got within a half of a mile from the depot going around a curve in the tracks.

The passengers watched as the outlaw stepped off the steps from the platform to the ground from the slow moving train.

He hurried over to a blood bay gelding being held by another man under a large red oak almost fifty yards from the tracks. The thief handed the sack to the horse holder, stuck his foot in the stirrup and swung into the saddle.

The two road agents spurred their mounts off to the north, with a yell, "Yee-haw."

They galloped out of view of the passengers on the train as it slowed further rounding the curve to the south.

"Good haul?" asked the young man who had been holding his horse as they rode away.

Duce Walton grinned. "You could say so. Boss man's information was right on…The courier was on that train…just like he said."

The children were all exiting the school house for the end of the school day—it was three in the afternoon.

A man in a dark sack cloth suit, wearing a black, uncreased tall crown hat with a red-tail hawk feather stuck into a quill and bead hat band, rode up to the back of the school on a grulla mare—leading a lineback dun. He reined up, stepped down and tied the horses to a hitching rail near the back door. The dust cloud he had generated billowed up behind him, and then began to settle.

Chickasaw Lighthorse, *Nashoba Hommá*, climbed the four steps to the stoop and knocked.

Silke opened the door. "Red Wolf! Let me guess, they hit again."

"Uhh…Wichita train. Got KATY payroll. Knew the man carryin' money was on train."

"Had to be someone on the inside that tipped him off…Same guy?"

"Uhh, him Gentleman Bandit…Kill conductor. Passengers identify from poster…Duce Walton."

Her jaw muscles flexed as Silke ground her teeth. "That's new…Murderin' bastard," she said.

Red Wolf nodded. "Man try grab gun...Not wise."

Silke shook her head as her three month old black wolf-dog pup, Bear Dog, crawled out from under her desk when she and Red Wolf came inside. "I'm goin' to catch him, God as my witness...He's mine. Been on his tail since the Tackett gang killed momma and daddy...He's the only one that hasn't paid the piper."

She had already changed from her schoolmarm outfit to her trail clothing—blue denim pants with a tan leather seat insert, dark burgundy three-button shirt and blue denim jacket. She had ordered a set of doeskins like Bone and Loraine wore, but hadn't gotten them yet. They were being custom made for her by Deputy US Marshal Fiona Flynn's grandmother in Tahlequah, Cherokee Nation.

Silke was in expectation of *Nashoba Hommá's* arrival and had released her long reddish-blond tresses from the constraining bun at the back of her head to a thick, loose, single braid that draped over her left shoulder. There was a beaded narrow leather strap around the end of the braid—a gift from Deputy US Marshal Fiona Miller Flynn.

SILKE JUSTICE

Silke Justice had been hired by the Missouri-Kansas-Texas Railroad through the Pinkerton National Detective Agency to track down Walton for a rash of train robberies across north Texas and the southern Indian Nations.

She had gotten her friend and mentor, Red Wolf, on loan from the Chickasaw Lighthorse Police force because Duce's trail often led back across the Red and into the Chickasaw Nation.

"You leave school, now?" asked Red Wolf.

She nodded. "The regular teacher is due back tomorrow from visiting her momma in Denton, who was ill, so I'm good to go...Where did the tracks lead?"

"Get off train outside Wichita Falls. Someone there with horse as usual...Head north, cross Red into Oklahoma Territory at Thornberry."

Silke nodded. "What I was afraid of...Knew KATY was tryin' to sneak the money to Wichita Falls with an undercover courier instead of an armed shipment in the express car...'cause that hadn't worked very well in the past...Somebody in the know told that scum."

She hesitated a moment, and then continued, "Need to find out where they're makin' the hand off…and to who…We get Duce Walton, they'll just get somebody else to do their dirty work. Need to cut the head off the snake."

§§§

CHAPTER TWO

DENISON, TEXAS
KATY OFFICE

"Mister Barksdale, I'm Silke Justice, Pinkerton National Detective Agency." She opened her small black leather wallet to show her brass badge and identification card to the district manager for KATY railroad. "This is Chickasaw Lighthorse, Red Wolf."

"Been expecting you Miss Justice. Got a

telegram from the St. Louis office that you were coming," said the portly man with thinning gray hair and mutton-chop whiskers.

Vernon Barksdale opened a humidor on his desk, removed a dark Cuban cigar and snipped the ends off with a silver cutter. He picked up a small pewter replica of a steam locomotive by Wedgwood, pressed a lever on the back which sparked a flame from the engine's smoke stack.

He ran the fire up and down the length of the expensive cigar to warm it and finally held it to the end, rotating the cigar until it was uniformly lit. Barksdale puffed on it several times and exhaled a blue smoke ring over his head, watching in satisfaction as it floated upward.

"I can't tell you how devastating the loss of that payroll is to the KATY, Miss Justice...This is the third time in the last two months...It has to stop!" He pounded the top of his desk.

"Yes sir, we at Pinkertons share your concern an' I can assure you we will get to the bottom of it...We know that the robber has been the same man...one Duce Walton, a known criminal, bank robber, tobyman, and murderer."

"Yes, yes, yes, but how do we stop him?" He took another draw from his cigar, exhaled a big cloud of smoke toward the ceiling and looked at the glowing end in his hand as if he were studying the burn pattern.

"We find out who he's gettin' his orders from."

"You mean he's not doing this on his own?"

"Not likely. He apparently knows when and how the payroll is being carried...I will find out how." Her blue eyes took on a flinty shade.

He cleared his throat and leaned back in his burgundy Spanish leather executive chair and looked at her and Red Wolf. "How can just a mere woman catch a murderous robber?...What is your agency thinking?"

Silke's eyes flashed momentarily as she slowly got to her feet and placed her hands on the front of his polished cherrywood desk and leaned over the top.

Her voice got soft and she looked straight into his right eye—the master eye, "Mister Barksdale...I want you to listen real close...The founder of the Pinkerton National Detective agency, Allen Pinkerton, personally hired a woman in 1856 by the name of Kate Warne. She not only was a heroine of the Civil War as a spy for the Union, but also became one of the agency's most decorated and effective detectives. She was able to ferret out information from places that it was impossible for male detectives to gain access to..." She added slowly, "I do the same."

Silke paused, straightened up and put her hands on her shapely hips. "Just a mere woman?...Honey, I'm an awesome, redheaded, Southern belle, with a dash of bulldog, a splash of gator, a double measure of sass, a hell of a left hook...and I can shoot the flies off a bull's ass at fifty yards...Does *that* answer your final question?"

Barksdale dropped his cigar from his mouth to his lap. He jumped up trying to brush the fire from the lit end of the cigar from his tailor-made striped pants before it burnt a hole.

"Oh, damn, oh, damn."

Silke got a wry grin and turned to Red Wolf. "Let's get the hell out of here...got work to do."

The district manager was still trying to stomp out the hot embers that had fallen from his lap to the expensive oriental carpet under his desk as Silke and Red Wolf exited.

SILKE JUSTICE

SKEANS BOARDING HOUSE
GAINESVILLE, TEXAS

"Duce's tracks led to the Red, and then into the Oklahoma Territory," Silke told Bone, Loraine and Padrino in the parlor of the boarding house. "And now, here's the interestin' part…he circled around into the Chickasaw Nation an' came back across the river at Heaton's Ferry just downstream of Red River Station in Montague County."

"Why do you suppose he did that?" asked Loraine, the 5'3" Hispanic beauty asked as she turned her back to the roaring fire in the fireplace.

"My best guess is to throw anybody tryin' to track him off," said Silke as she took a sip of her coffee. "What he doesn't know is I have Chickasaw Lighthorse *Nashoba Hommá*, Red Wolf, trackin' him."

"Bass said he was a hellova tracker," said Bone.

Darrell Ulysses Bone and Loraine Rodriguez Bone were a husband and wife team of detectives from 2019 trapped here in 1899 when they accidently went through an ancient Amerindian portal in late 1898.

23

The 6'8" Bone's godfather, Padrino, a retired Master Gunnery Sergeant from the Marine Corps, had joined them through the same ancient Amerindian portal in the Brazos River area in Palo Pinto County near what is today, Possum Kingdom Lake.

He used a special power crystal from a large meteor impact, known as a *moldivite* crystal. The eons old crystal had been given to him by a Navajo Shaman years earlier. He was able to use it to enter the electromagnetic vortex to catapult him into the past also.

Silke nodded. "He can even tell the difference between a stud, geldin' or mare tracks." She grinned as she reached down and scratched Bear Dog's ears while he slept at her feet. "I still don't understand how he does it."

"Do you have any leads on the robber?" asked Padrino.

"Not a one, except that it's Duce Walton…You know, the one member of Big John Tackett's gang that got away?…Bass said he an' the three with him killed those two drummers on the road south of Dougherty for no reason."

"I know, I was with him…It was definitely a needless killing. When Bass and I came up on the scene, they had made the two men strip to their underwear, shot them, and then burned their wagon…Despicable," said Padrino.

"Ah, him…Disappeared into the Oklahoma Territority, didn't he?" asked Bone.

"He did," answered Silke. "Then he starts robbin' trains…but only the KATY in the Nations an' Texas."

"Wonder why just them?" asked Padrino.

Silke looked at each one. "He only robs the trains carryin' the KATY payroll."

"How does he know?"

"That my dear Loraine is the fly in the buttermilk…Walton ain't the sharpest knife in the drawer…There has to be someone on the inside funnelin' him the information an' I fully intend on findin' out who it is…KATY has hired the agency to deal with this, an' that's me."

"You're going to let him lead you to the leak," said Bone.

"Exactly…Then I'll take care of that murderin' trash…my way."

Ken Farmer

The front door to the stately three story red brick Queen Anne style boarding house opened and two men entered. They both unbuckled their gunbelts and hung them along with their hats on the hall tree.

"Bodie Hickman," Bone said as he looked from the parlor into the foyer and got to his feet.

The big rawboned, redheaded, Texas Ranger strode into the parlor with his friend who was about two inches shorter than Bodie's 6'2", holding his hand out to Bone. They shook and Bodie gave Loraine a brief hug, and shook Padrino's hand too, then he turned to his companion.

"Ya'll, this here is Ranger Riley Boston up from Austin...We joined up 'bout the same time, five years ago. Riley, this is Detective Bone, his wife, Detective Loraine Bone and Bone's godfather, Padrino...and I'm afraid I don't know this lovely lady." He indicated Silke.

Bear Dog woke up from his nap and looked at Silke, and then at Bodie, who was speaking.

"Yes, you do, you just don't know it," replied Bone.

"Huh?"

"Bodie, this is Pinkerton Detective Silke Justice."

"Oh, by ginger, you're right...Have heard of you, Miss Justice," replied Bodie.

"So have I...You've got quite a reputation...Uh, Miss Justice," commented Riley as he nodded his head at the beautiful strawberry blond, clearly taken.

Loraine didn't miss the instant electricity between Silke and the broad shouldered, narrow waisted, young ranger with a full brown mustache.

She smiled, wrinkling her small freckled nose slightly and showing her white even teeth. "Well, to start with, it's Silke an' from all Bone and Loraine have told me of you an' your lovely wife, Annabel, I must say I've really been lookin' forward to meetin' ya'll." She turned to Riley. "An' you're well known to the Pinkertons also...Ranger Boston." Silke held out her hand.

Boston stammered until he found his tongue and shook her hand, holding it a little longer than was necessary. "Uh...I...Uh, yes...Mis...uh, Silke. Heard of you too...'Spect most everbody has...Just wad'nt expectin' you to be so..."

"So what, Riley?" Bodie grinned at his friend's discomfort.

"So, young an'...an'..."

27

"Oh, spit it out Ranger Boston," said Loraine. "So pretty." A big grin spread across her face also.

"Uh…yessum…that too," Riley managed to get out and blushed as he quickly looked down at the polished hardwood floor.

Bodie shook his head. "Gonna have to tie kerosene rags around yer ankles to keep the sugar ants off." He slapped Riley's back.

Silke's tanned face took on a distinct shade of pink, also.

"Aw, come on, Bodie," Boston punched Bodie on the arm.

The proprietor, Faye Skeans, came down the stairs with Bodie's blond-haired wife, Annabel, from Alabama, and entered the parlor.

"Your room is ready, Silke, Annabel gave me a hand…Who's your friend, Bodie?" asked the sixty year old attractive dark blond widow after she exchanged glances and smiles with Padrino.

Introductions were made again by Bodie.

"Do you have another room, Faye?" Bodie asked.

"Got one left." She looked at Riley. "If you want it Ranger Boston."

He grinned and nodded. "Yessum, you don't mind…Looks like I'm goin' to be here a spell."

"Love havin' a full house. Good thing I fixed an extra big pot of chicken an' dumplins."

"Chicken an' dumplins? Oh, wow, my favorite," exclaimed Bone.

Bear Dog yipped and spun around in a circle.

"His too," added Bone.

"Everything is your favorite, Bone," commented Loraine.

The giant of a man shrugged. "Well?" He lifted his head and sniffed. "Is that…"

"Yes, Bone, it's a floating crust, peach-apple cobbler," interrupted Faye.

"Oh, my, I have died and gone to heaven," replied Bone.

Faye grinned and turned to Boston. "Take it you have an assignment up here, Ranger?" asked Faye.

"Yessum, gotta catch a train robber."

Silke cocked her head.

§§§

CHAPTER THREE

DEXTER, TEXAS
SUGAR HILL SALOON

Two well-dressed men sat at a table in the far corner of the dimly lit saloon. Each had a four ounce gill tumbler in front of them, two-thirds filled with an amber liquid.

Identical brown leather valises were in one of the extra bow chairs at the square table.

SILKE JUSTICE

"Just so you know, Walton, the Pinkerton Detective Agency has assigned one of their detectives to track you down…A woman…Silke Justice."

Duce snorted. "Damn woman don't bother me none. You keep coming with the good information on the payrolls an' I'll keep pickin' 'em up."

"The details of the next shipment is in that valise along with your cut of the last one. Just don't do anything stupid again like killing another employee." The man shook his head. "Not bright, not bright at all…Bring the rangers down on us."

"Couldn't be helped, he grabbed my gun," said Walton.

"See that it doesn't happen again," the other man ordered as he got to his feet, picked up one of the valises and headed across the room toward the door.

Duce watched him leave, picked up his glass and threw back what was left, and then he did the same with the other glass.

SKEANS BOARDING HOUSE

"You mean we're workin' on the same case?"

31

Silke looked across the dinner table at the handsome young ranger. "So it would seem, Riley, so it would seem."

"Son of a gun, don't that beat all," he grinned as he shook his head and stared intently at her blue eyes. "So, what do you know, so far?"

"Not a lot, except that it's all been the same man, a Duce Walton…real curley wolf.

Ten minutes later, Silke, Bone, and Loraine finished telling Ranger Boston what they knew about Walton, the chase and elimination of the Big John Tackett gang up in the Nations last month.

Silke took a sip of her after-dinner coffee and leaned back in her chair. "What I don't quite understand is we know he's a cold blooded, often indiscriminate killer, but yet, he's only killed one person since he started hittin' the trains."

"What's the count to date on robberies?" asked Riley.

"The one last week was number five…Three up in the Nations and two now in Texas…All in about a month," replied Silke.

"Looks like the Rangers didn't waste any time once he started hittin' trains in Texas," commented Bone.

"I'd say," added Padrino.

"Anybody need a coffee refill or another bowl of cobbler?...Jethro?" asked Faye as she came through the two way hinged door to the kitchen.

"That sure is good cobbler, sweet Faye...don't mind if I do," replied Padrino.

She winked at him and started to head back to the kitchen.

"Don't have to ask me twice, Faye," said Bone.

"Or me," added Bodie.

"You might as well make it four, ma'am," commented Riley with a big grin.

"I'll help you, Faye," said Loraine as she pushed her chair from the table.

Faye smiled. "Always appreciated, Missus Bone."

"I'm not lettin' your pants out again, mister," Annabel addressed her husband, Bodie.

"It's like Marshal McGann always says, honey, 'Don't ever turn down Faye's cobbler'," said Bodie.

"You, remember, he only says that when Angie's not around," retorted Annabel. "Of course you can also start wearing bib overalls." She giggled.

"Don't think the Rangers would go for that," said Bone with a grin.

"Good point, there big man," replied Bodie. "Say, anybody for goin' down to the Painted Lady for a beer? I'll go the first round."

"Works for me," answered Bone.

"Bone's about beer like he is cobbler," said Loraine as she came back through the door from the kitchen with Faye as they brought four bowls of cobbler and set them in front of the men.

"Well, as I recall, love, you never turned down an opportunity to gather for a libation at the Governor's Lounge," replied Bone.

"What's the Governor's Lounge?" asked Riley.

"It's a cop hangout back home," said Bone.

He and everyone in the dining room except Ranger Boston exchanged glances. "Oh, he doesn't know, does he?"

"Doesn't know what?" replied Riley.

"Just as well tell him, honey, if he's going to be here a while," offered Loraine.

Bone took a deep breath. "All right, grab your butt Ranger, this may blow your socks off."

"Huh?"

Thirty minutes later, Bone, Loraine, and Padrino finished telling Ranger Boston all about them being time travelers and from when...including about Lucy being a stranded alien when her spacecraft crashed at Aurora, Texas in 1897.

"So, that's the name of that tune, Ranger...Uh...You can breath now," said Bone.

Riley blinked his brown eyes a couple of times, took a deep breath and looked at Silke. "You already knew about this, too?"

She gave him a big grin and nodded.

Ranger Boston looked around the table with a blank look on his face. "Don't know which is harder to believe...ya'll being from the future or your friend Annuna, or Lucy, as you call her, being from another planet...Think I'm ready for that drink now."

Everyone smiled.

"Thought you'd never bring it up," said Bone as he slid back from the table.

"Ya'll go ahead, hear? Think I'll stay an' read to the twins. I've started on *Treasure Island* an' they're expectin' the next chapter before they go nite-nite, bless their hearts," commented Annabel as she looked at Bodie. "An' don't be out late, mister."

Bodie grinned and looked at the others. "That little Alabama gal will snatch me baldheaded if I am."

She gave him a sweet kiss on the lips. "Uh-huh…an' don't you forget it."

PAINTED LADY SALOON

"This is as nice as any saloon we got down in Austin," said Riley as they came through the batwing doors after opening the tall double doors that were normally closed during the winter months.

He remove his gray Stetson, ran his fingers through his wavy brown hair and looked up over his head fourteen feet at the embossed tin ceiling and multiple ceiling fans. They were all driven from one electric motor by a long single belt that ran to each one.

There were four chandelier type lights spaced evenly across the fifty by sixty room. The last thirty feet of the ninety foot long two story brick building was taken up by the kitchen, storeroom, and male and female privies.

There was also a large dressing room for the twenty foot wide by twelve foot deep stage with an upright piano behind a full-length purple velvet curtain. It was pulled to the sides and a painted canvas backdrop depicting many local business advertisements hung at the back.

"Big round table or stand at the bar?" Bone pointed at the thirty-five foot long San Francisco style ornate hand-carved bar along the south side with a fifteen foot gilded, beveled mirror in the center of the back bar.

"Let's do a table," suggested Silke, much easier to visit than constantly being jostled at the bar.

There was a good mix of customers in the upscale saloon that many compared to the Bird Cage Theater in Tombstone—at least until it closed in 1889. It was also similar to Wyatt Earp's Oriental Saloon, also in Tombstone, in 1880.

There were business types and gamblers at the gaming tables. Cowboys from the many ranches around the county mostly lined up at the bar.

They found an empty round table near the center of the room that would seat the six of them. Riley pulled out a chair for Silke.

"Why thank you, kind sir," she replied as she sat down.

Loraine stood by her chair, after seeing Riley's chivalry, tapping her foot and looking at Bone with her arms folded over her ample bosom.

He finally noticed after taking his usual perusal of the room. "Oh, sorry, Babe." Bone pulled the chair away from the table and bowed. "Here you go, Double D."

Loraine backhanded him across his broad chest. "Damn you, Bone."

He giggled and sat down beside her.

Riley leaned over to Silke. "They like this all the time?"

She grinned and nodded. "Pretty much…They were partners on the police force for four years before they got married."

Boston returned a knowing nod. "You can tell."

A tall attractive brunette waitress came over to their table. She was dressed in a typical saloon girl low cut dress, but as a costume. None of the servers in the saloon worked as girls of the line in the Chickasaw Parlor House bordello upstairs.

"What are ya'll havin'...Hey, Bone, Bodie, Loraine, haven't seen ya'll in a coon's age."

"Been kinda busy, Brandi, takin' care of law breakers an' outlaws on the scout."

"Uh-huh...Who are your friends?" She flashed a big grin at them.

Bone made the introductions of Silke, Riley, and Padrino."

"Glad to meetcha," Brandi replied.

"Ladies," said Bodie.

"What do you have cold in bottles, Brandi?" asked Silke.

"Lone Star an' Pearl."

"Pearl for me, then," she replied.

"That's good," said Loraine.

"Lone Star," added Bone.

"Me, too," commented Padrino.

"Three," said Bodie.

"Four," finished Riley, holding up four fingers.

"Be right back. Don't ya'll goway, now, hear?" Brandi turned and sashayed toward the bar.

Bone grinned as he watched her. "Only southern gals know how to sashay...She reminds me of Peach Presley back home."

"She does, doesn't she," replied Loraine.

"Who's Peach Presley?" asked Bodie.

"A crackerjack forensics technician, from Georgia, in our department, back...or forward in our time," answered Loraine. "If you argue with Peach and she calls you 'precious' and 'sweetheart' in the same sentence...you better start ducking."

There was a commotion at the door as five cowboys from the Circle W burst through. They had apparently already made a stop at the White Elephant Saloon next door.

"Uh-oh," said Bone as he looked up.

"What is it?" asked Silke.

"Trouble...with a capital T," responded Bone.

She turned in her chair to look at the front door where Bone indicated...

§§§

CHAPTER FOUR

DEXTER HOTEL

Duce Walton and his partner, Goose Merkins, sat in slat-back chairs around a small square table in their room at the end of the hall on the second floor of the shiplap-sided hotel. The outside stairway to the ground was at their end.

"Here's yer cut, Goose." Walton counted out ten one hundred dollar bank notes in front of the man.

Duce pulled out a sheet of paper from the leather valise and unfolded it on the table.

"That the next job?" asked Merkins.

Walton held up his hand while he read. "Uh-huh." Duce nodded and grinned. "Next payroll will be on the northbound from Denison to Atoka, up in the Nations, in two days."

"Where do we hit it?"

"Between Armstrong and Caddo, just south of Clear Boggy Creek. She has to stop at Caddo fer water." He looked up at Goose. "Gonna be in the express car this time…with guards. Need the rest of the boys fer thisun."

"All of 'em?"

Duce nodded. "All of 'em."

PAINTED LADY SALOON

The five working cowboys burst through the front doors like they owned the place, laughing and shoving each other, obviously already well lubricated.

Rube Jolley, the bartender, a heavyset man in his forties, looked up with no small degree of consternation on his face. He pulled out old Betsy, a well-used baseball bat from underneath the bar, laid it on the back bar, and then turned back around and wiped up an imaginary spill on the top of the polished bar with a white towel.

Timothy McPherson, the strikingly handsome thirty-five year old owner of the Painted Lady, sat at a nearby table with an attractive young blond, interviewing her for a job as a stage singer-entertainer. He glanced over at Bone's table, knowing the big man and Loraine were deputy sheriffs, and Bodie was a Texas Ranger.

Bone nodded at McPherson and kept his eyes on the rowdy cowboys as they were making room for themselves at the bar by nudging other patrons out of the way.

Several of the disgruntled customers started to say something, but then thought better of it and moved on down the bar. All but one, that is.

A thick necked, blocky man refused to make room for the cowboys and continued to drink his draft beer.

The self-appointed leader of the group, a broad-shouldered, big armed man, forcibly nudged the town blacksmith to the side. He glanced at his friends and grinned.

The big man next to him turned and grabbed the cowboy's shoulder, turning him away from the bar.

The cowboy drew his Colt and pressed it against the town blacksmith's stomach and pushed the man backward. "How 'bout you jest move down the bar an' let some real men order their drinks?"

Bone started to get to his feet when Silke interrupted him, placing her hand on his arm.

"Let me handle this, Bone. Want to try some of that Kung Fu stuff Loraine's been showin' me." She set her hat on the table and headed to the bar.

"Go get 'em, kid," Bone replied with a grin and sat back down.

"Don't forget, Silke, use their movements against them," cautioned Loraine, sotto voce.

She stepped up behind the cowboy. "You know, slick, I don't see a single man in your whole bunch."

The stunned wrangler turned and looked down at her. "What?…Who the hell are you, lady?…Or is that the term I should use?" He holstered his gun with a sneer and looked down at her riding pants.

"It doesn't matter what you use, because I don't like your company...Do you or any of your...associates know what soap and water are?...Ya'll could give a manure wagon a run...Phew!" She turned her head to the side.

"Listen you little split-tail..." He reached forward and laid his hand on Silke's left shoulder to push her backward. She grabbed his wrist, placed her thumb on his scaphoid bone, near the base of his thumb and pressed down.

The cowboy cried out as his knees buckled with the pain.

"I don't like that term, mister, I want an apology...right now...Don't advise waitin' too long." She pressed a little harder.

He cried out again. "Awright, awright, calf-rope, calf-rope...I'm sorry."

"What? I didn't hear that," Silke said.

He almost screamed, "I'm sorry."

Silke released her hand and crossed her arms over her bosom.

"You gonna let her do that to you, Mule?" asked one of the other cowboys with a snicker.

Loraine got to her feet back at the table.

"Hell, no," said Mule as he swung a haymaker at Silke's head.

She ducked, grabbed his elbow, used his two hundred pounds of momentum, jerked his face down and forward into the top of the bar.

He hit with a *splat,* breaking his nose and splattering blood across the top of the bar in the process. He slid to the floor and collapsed on the brass foot rail.

The man who had egged Mule on, stepped to Silky, his fist already in motion. It never reached her, however, because he collapsed to the floor with a scream as Loraine side-kicked his knee with the heel of her foot. She looked at Silke, and they exchanged grins.

One of the other men drew his pistol, but Silke slapped his hand down toward the floor where it discharged through his foot and on into the sawdust covered hardwood floor. He too screamed, falling backward to his butt and grabbing his bleeding foot.

Loraine pinched and twisted the fourth's man lower lip between her thumb and forefinger, pulling him forward toward Silke. The Pink spun around, backfisted him, smashing his nose and dropping him to the floor like a girl's rag doll.

The fifth man held his hands up in the air and backed toward the front door. When he reached the end of the bar, he whirled around and almost ran into Town Marshal Kenneth Farmer who was coming in the door.

The square-jawed lawman poked the cowboy in the stomach with his bull penis cane, stopping him in his tracks. He walked forward poking him a few more times, backing the cowboy back to the others.

"Now what's all this then?" the stocky lawman asked as he lowered his cane back to the ground to support himself.

Marshal Farmer had shattered his right leg when he fell from the judge's tower during the Great Gainesville Horse Race after being shot by Tom Story's gang robbing the administration tent four years earlier.

"Oh, just a little misunderstanding, Marshal," said Loraine. "Seems the Circle W boys left their manners at the ranch," said Loraine.

Farmer looked at the four men moaning on the floor of the saloon, then at Loraine and finally at Silke.

"You two did this?" he asked.

Loraine and Silke exchanged glances and shrugged.

"Seemed like the thing to do at the time…Hate rudeness, won't tolerate it," commented Silke.

"And just who might you be?" asked Farmer.

"Marshal, this is Pinkerton Detective Silke Justice."

"You Miller Justice's daughter?" he asked.

"Yes, sir," Silke replied, nodding.

"Sorry for your loss…Admired your folks…Heard of you," responded Farmer.

"Thank you, sir," said Silke.

Marshal Farmer looked at Timothy McPherson who had walked forward. "Want to press charges against this riffraff, Tim?"

The dark-haired man with silver temples smiled, showing his even, white teeth. "Oh, I don't think so, Marshal…Believe these boys have suffered enough." He looked down at Mule. There was still a trickle of blood running from his broken nose. "Isn't that a fact?"

"Yessir, shore is," he replied with a distinct nasal tone as he staggered to his feet, pulled his bandana from his neck and held it to his nose to staunch the flow.

"You boys going to behave in my saloon from now on?" McPherson asked.

Mule glanced at Silke, and then Loraine. "These little gals ain't gonna hurt us no more…air they?"

Silke grinned at the whipped cowboy. "Not as long as you play nice."

"Oh, yessum, count on it." He reached up and wiggled a loose front tooth with his fingers. "You an' this other lady here is she-bears in satin…Ya'll could raise blood blisters on a boot," Mule added, still with a nasal whine.

Loraine turned to the bartender. "Rube, give these boys a beer on our tab." She turned to the five cowboys. "Then ya'll go home…Hear?"

There were nods and mumbled, "Yes, ma'ams."

"And don't call me 'ma'am…understand? It's Deputy or Missus Bone."

"Yes, ma…Uh, Deputy."

"Uh…Missus Bone," the others replied as they got to their feet.

As one they turned toward the bar.

The man with the hole in his foot leaned heavily on one of his buddies. "Gotta git this foot took care of…Dang my melt…ruint a good pair of boots."

Silke and Loraine headed back to the table and took their seats.

Riley's mouth was hung open as he stared at Silke.

Bodie elbowed him in the side. "Better close your mouth, Riley, you're catchin' flies."

"Oh, right," he said as he blushed.

"You'll get used to it. You shoulda seen what Loraine did to Bone over in Jacksboro…an' she was just demonstratin' some moves," said Bodie.

"That's a fact, Jack," said Bone. "Take it from one who knows, you don't want to piss either one of them off."

Silke looked over at Loraine. "When is the next lesson?…Think I like that stuff."

Loraine grinned and nodded. "See, what did I tell you?…Tomorrow too soon?"

"Perfect," Silke replied.

Bone spoke up, "But, just remember, it only works when they're inside your danger zone…arm's length. Outside of that…" He patted his Smith and Wesson .50 caliber handgun.

"I follow that…Love to have me one of those." Silke's face lit up with a big grin as she looked at the hand cannon.

McPherson walked up to their table just as Brandi arrived with their beers on a tray. He turned to her. "All their drinks are on the house, Brandi…plus anything else they might want."

"That's really not necessary, Timothy," said Loraine. "Just doing our job…Oh, you haven't officially met. This is Detective Silke Justice and Texas Ranger Riley Boston."

"Very happy to meet you," he shook hands with Silke and made eye contact—their matching blue eyes connecting. "I heard Loraine say you were a Pinkerton over at the bar."

He nodded to her, released her hand, and then held his out to Riley. "It's a pleasure, Ranger. Always glad to meet friends of Bodie."

§§§

CHAPTER FIVE

SKEANS BOARDING HOUSE

The early morning sun sent red arrows across the eastern horizon, turning the few clouds first to red then to gold as the darkness was chased to the west.

Red Wolf knocked on the white gingerbread screen door. He waited a moment and started to knock again when the ornate wood main door with a frosted glass top opened.

"May I help you?" asked Faye.

"Red Wolf need see Silke Justice."

"Oh, yes, she's mentioned you, Red Wolf. Won't you come in?" She unlatched the screen door and pushed it open for him to enter.

"She's in the kitchen with some of my other boarders having coffee. Would you like a cup?"

Red Wolf grinned and nodded. "Yessum, please," he answered after he hung his black, tall crown, uncreased hat on the hall tree and followed her down the hall from the foyer to the kitchen.

Silke looked up from her cup and set it down on the breakfast table. "Red Wolf! Good to see you."

The Chickasaw Lighthorse nodded. "Uhhh, good see you, Silke Justice."

"Take anything in your coffee, Red Wolf?" asked Faye.

He grinned and nodded. "Uhhh, Red Wolf like sugar. Makes sweet."

She set the cup on the table along with the sugar bowl. "You can sugar it to suit you."

"Ya'll, this is my trail mentor, Chickasaw Lighthorse *Nashoba Hommá*...Red Wolf, meet Rangers Bodie Hickman and Riley Boston...and

Deputies Bone and his wife, Loraine Bone and Bone's godfather, Padrino."

Everyone at the table exchanged greetings with the Lighthorse.

"Bass Reeves had a lot of good things to say about you, Red Wolf," said Bone.

"Uhhh, Marshal Reeves good man. Him made part of Chickasaw tribe moons ago…Great warrior."

Red Wolf looked back to Silke as he sat down at the table. "That why Red Wolf here. Chickasaw Shaman *Anompoli Lawa* send to tell Silke Justice she is to be made Chickasaw warrior, also…Much great honor."

Silke's hand raised to her mouth. "Oh, my." Her sky blue eyes filled. "This is wonderful. You must tell *Anompoli Lawa* how much I appreciate this honor."

"Silke Justice must return with Red Wolf. She go through warrior ceremony."

She got a puzzled expression across her face. "Warrior ceremony? But, I'm…"

"He know. You show to be great warrior when kill Big John Tackett. Him enemy of Chickasaw many years, kill many Chickasaw, including women

54

and children. Good him die by Silke Justice hand…Great coup."

Silke dabbed her eyes with her napkin. "I was just doin' what needed to be done…He killed my mother and father."

Red Wolf head bobbed once. "Him need killing…Silke Justice no want go?"

"Oh, my goodness, no…I mean, yes, of course I'll come. When?"

"Now."

She looked at the others at the table. "Gracious…I…"

"Can we come and watch the ceremony?" asked Loraine.

"Close friends may watch part…not all." Red Wolf glanced at each of the others.

"Count me in," said Padrino.

"Me too," said Bodie.

"And me," added Riley.

"Where do we go?" asked Silke.

"Go to Marshal McGann property at what called Turner Falls on Honey Creek. Is sacred area to Chickasaw…Take afternoon train to Ardmore." Red Wolf took a spoon and added five heaping teaspoons of sugar to his coffee and stirred.

"Like coffee with your sugar, Red Wolf?" asked Bone with a grin.

"Uhhh, no have sugar when young. Find out what is after grown…Like."

Padrino also grinned. "You think?"

"Best get packed Missus Bone."

Loraine smiled. "I'll take care of it, Mister Bone."

"Wish I had my new buckskins Fiona's grandmother is makin' for me."

"*Anompoli Lawa* already contact her and having them sent to him so Chickasaw warrior beadwork be added for after ceremony."

"I don't need them for the ceremony?" asked Silke.

Red Wolf returned her look with a wordless stare. Silke swore she saw a twinkle in his dark brown eyes.

ARDMORE DEPOT, IT

The big locomotive blew steam as she braked to a stop at the red brick platform outside the wood depot building for the Gulf and Colorado Railroad.

Silke and the others grabbed their carpet bags, saddlebags and long guns and followed Red Wolf down the aisle to the door at the front of the car. She also led Bear Dog on a leather leash.

They stepped down to the platform and were met by a white-haired Chickasaw in a dark three piece suit and tall, uncreased black Stetson with a Red-Tail Hawk feather stuck in a bead and quill hat band.

"*Anompoli Lawa*, this Silke Justice," said Red Wolf.

"My dear, welcome, welcome." He embraced her. "I am also known as Doctor Winchester Ashalatubbi...I am a doctor of medicine, a doctor of divinity, as well as being Shaman for the Chickasaw Nation...You may call me either or both. *Anompoli Lawa* means 'He Who Talks to Many'." He flashed a big grin showing his strong white teeth.

"Jack will tell you that he can birth you, doctor over you, get you hitched, shoo away the evil spirits, and bury you...If need be," added Bone.

"So happy to meet you, *Anompoli Lawa*...Since you already know everyone else, this is Texas Ranger Riley Boston...We have been assigned to the same crime or series of crimes against the KATY."

Winchester stuck out his hand, Riley took it and they shook. Boston marveled at the elder Chickasaw's strength of grip.

"My pleasure, Doctor Ashalatubbi."

"This is my nurse, Yellow Bird. She came to take care of an errand for me."

They all exchanged greetings with the Chickasaw woman.

A colored porter in a white jacket walked up. "Package for you Doctor Ashalatubbi." He handed him a brown paper wrapped bundle tied with string. "It be from a Singing Moon in Tahlequah, Cherokee Nation."

"Ah, your deerskins, my dear, but, you may not have them yet." He handed the package to Yellow Bird. "She will drop them off to our ladies to finish. I'm sure Red Wolf has already told you," said Winchester.

"Yes, I understand. It's fine," replied Silke. "I'm looking forward to seeing them when they're done."

"Shall we go? I have a carriage out front. Be a little crowded, but we'll be fine," commented Winchester. "It's about twenty-five miles out to

Jack and Angie's. They'll be expecting us for supper."

"So, we won't be doing the ceremony today?" asked Silke.

"Oh, goodness no, child. It's rather lengthy. We'll start in the morning."

"Red Wolf get horse and come out in morning, *Anompoli Lawa*."

"That's fine, *Nashoba Hommá*...This way folks."

He led the way to the front of the depot to a large black Phaeton carriage with facing seats.

"Be more room if I ride up on the driver's bench with you, Doc. Don't you think?"

"Excellent idea, Bone. Yes, indeed, excellent idea," Winchester replied.

They loaded up and Winchester flicked the ribbons over the rumps of a matched set of sorrel Standardbred geldings. "Come up, boys." He clucked at them as they started off at a trot.

Bear Dog lay down at Silke's feet on the floorboard between the seats.

Two and a half hours later, the Phaeton turned down the private road down into Honey Creek valley where Jack and Angie's large log home was built about a hundred yards downstream from the seventy-seven foot high Turner Falls.

They farmed about fifteen acres up on top of the ridge above the house for their own vegetables along with grain and alfalfa for the livestock. There was an orchard down close to the house with apple, peach, fig, and plum trees.

About three hundred yards from the house there were two large wolf-dogs, a white one and a black one, sitting in the middle of the road.

"Look," exclaimed Silke.

"That's Son and *Nita*," said Bone. "That offspring of Boy, the spirit wolf, and the pup that Aurali Red rescued…the ones we told you about."

Silke smiled and nodded.

"They always know when someone is coming and will meet us at this very spot…and lead us to the house," said Loraine.

Bear Dog had gotten to his feet and climbed up in Silke's lap so he could see. He yipped at Son and *Nita*. They woofed back.

"Let the pup down, and he can run along with them," said Winchester.

"Do you think he'll be all right? They won't..."

Winchester grinned. "Oh, I think it will be fine, go ahead and set him on the road...Whoa up there, boys." He pulled back on the reins.

Silke undid his leash and let the pup jump to the ground. He immediately ran up to the front of the horses, wiggling and waggling his tail. He licked Son and *Nita's* muzzles, and then fell over on his back, still wiggling.

Son and *Nita* sniffed of Bear Dog, and then licked him in return. He jumped up and the three took off up the road in the direction of the house.

The pup was doing his best to keep up. Son and *Nita* both looked back and adjusted their speed accordingly. At four months of age, he was still a bit gangly and clumsy.

Anompoli Lawa smiled as he clucked to the geldings again. "See?"

Ranger Boston glanced to their left at the gurgling, crystal clear, Honey Creek that paralleled the road. "This is really a beautiful area."

"Wait till you see the falls just past the house," said Bone.

They rounded the corner and pulled up in front of the large log home with a wide wraparound porch across the front and one side. The roof was of standing-seam galvanized metal.

Son, *Nita*, and Bear Dog ran up to the fence.

Jack, Angie, five year old Baby Sarah, and twelve year old Aurali Red were all standing on the porch waiting.

Winchester reined the team to a stop at the white picket fence around the front yard next to a hitching rail.

"How did they know we were here?" asked Silke.

"Son and *Nita* told them," said Winchester.

§§§

CHAPTER SIX

MCGANN HOME
ARBUCKLE MOUNTAINS, IT

"*Shee-ah*, the McGanns," said Winchester as he stepped down from the carriage.

"*Shee-ah, Anompoli Lawa*," replied Jack and Angie.

"An' ye be just in time, Uncle. There's a big baked ham, with applesauce, I just took out of me oven with candied sweet potatoes, put by peas, and buttermilk cornbread, I'll be settin' on me table," said Angie. "An' it's pecan-sweet potato pies with a bourbon glaze I made special for Bone."

The big man grabbed his chest with his right hand and staggered slightly, imitating a heart attack. "Oh, oh...I can die happy...That's my all-time favorite."

Loraine grinned and shook her head. "I gotta make a list."

Angie turned to Jack. "See to me uncle's horses, love, while I help our guests unload their traps."

"Right on it, Angiedarlin'," said the stocky, broad-shouldered, mustachioed, lawman as he went down the six steps from the porch to the ground and walked along the flagstones to the gate in the fence.

Jack undid the latch and swung the gate inward. The three wolf-dogs darted in, ran up the steps and onto the porch to the girls.

Baby Sarah and Aurali Red squealed and jumped up and down.

"A puppy," said Baby Sarah as she knelt down and hugged Bear Dog. The half-grown pup responded with multiple kisses to her little freckled face as Son and *Nita* joined in for their share of attention.

"Let's take 'em for a walk down to the falls, Baby Sarah," suggested Aurali Red shaking her long flaming red curls up and down.

"Oh, yes, let's do," replied the small blond.

The two girls dashed for the gate and headed to the path along the creek that led to the tallest falls in the Indian Nations and Oklahoma Territory.

"Ye be careful, girls. Don't get too close to the creek," yelled Angie. "An' be back in fifteen minutes...Supper's on the table."

"Yes, Ma," they both yelled back as they disappeared down the path with the two black and one white wolf-dogs running beside them. "It's a pack we have now."

Jack turned to Bone. "Those two blackuns could be brothers, 'ceptin' fer the eyes...*Nita* with his gold ones and the pup with his blues." He looked at Silke. "What do you call him?"

"Bear Dog...It's like he knows what you're sayin' when he looks at you...Oh, I'm Silke Justice." She held out her hand and smiled.

Jack grinned back. "Figured as much." He turned as Angie walked up to help with the bags.

Ken Farmer

"This is my lovely bride, Angiedarlin'…She's my *acushla*."

"What's an '*acushla*'?" asked Silke.

"It's Gaelic for 'pulse of my heart'."

"Oh, how sweet," said Silke.

"Oh, go on with ye blarney, man of the house," said Angie as she swatted his butt with her dishtowel that had been draped over her right shoulder.

He grinned and kissed her on the cheek, and then took the line attached to the headstall of the lead Saddlebred, turned them, and led them to the barn to unhook, feed, water, and give them a good rubdown after the long trip from town.

"I'll give you a hand, Jack," commented Bodie as he handed his gear to Riley and fell in beside the venerable marshal.

"Angie…Know you haven't met, this is Silke Justice, Bone's godfather, Padrino, and Texas Ranger Riley Boston," said Loraine.

The redheaded Irish woman cocked her head at her beautiful Hispanic counterpart. "And it's guessin' I am ye'll be tellin' me how it was he came from the future to join man mountain an' yeself, later?"

"Of course…I'm sure Red Wolf or Winchester has already filled you in about Silke?"

"They have, an' it's lookin' forward to the ceremony that me uncle will be conductin' tomorrow, we are.

"Tiz a great honor the Chickasaw Nation is bestowing on ye, lovely lassie." She hugged Silke and looked at her strawberry-blond hair in its usual single, loose, long braid, draped over her left shoulder and her porcelain skin. "It's thinking I am that ye've got a bit of the Irish in ye?"

Silke smiled and nodded. "Thank you, yes, Angie…my maternal grandmother was from County Cork…She had hair like yours."

"Aye, and ye have the look, too."

She nodded again. "Not sure why I deserve this great honor, but I'm not about to refuse it. It think that would be very rude of me."

"Yes, it's looking at it that way the Chickasaw would," replied Angie. "Now, let's go inside and get ye settled in before supper an' ye can decide if ye want coffee or sweet tea with ye supper."

"Already decided," said Bone as they climbed the steps. "Sweet tea in a quart Mason jar."

"It's just like me Jack, ye are then, Bone."

Angie showed everyone where they would be sleeping in the large house. Padrino, Doctor Ashalatubbi, Bodie, and Riley, would be sleeping on the screened-in porch on the east side of the house.

They all dropped their gear, washed up at the wash basin on the wide shelf where the white porcelain water bucket hung. It was located at the end of the screened-in porch next to the kitchen.

Everyone took a seat at the long plank-oak trestle table in the dining room. There were high-backed, calf-hide bottom, slat back, chairs at each end and one side. A long bench ran the length of the other side. The table was covered with a white linen table cloth.

Jack and Bodie came through the door from the porch where they also had washed up after grooming and feeding Winchester's horses.

"Mmm, smells good, Angiedarlin'."

"That's an understatement if there ever was one, Jack," said Bodie.

"Oh, my, yes, it does smell delic…"

Silke was interrupted by a high-pitched scream from the path to the falls.

"The *leanai*!" Angie yelled and darted to the front door, followed by everyone else.

Bone rapidly took the lead of the group after they left the yard as he charged like a freight train around the corner and down the trail.

He held up his hand for everyone behind him to stop as the girls were standing frozen in the middle of the path. The three wolf-dogs were in front of them, the hair was standing up along their back as they were all snarling at a large, dark, cottonmouth coiled up in the path. Its head was raised to strike and the mouth wide open showing the white insides from which the snake got its name.

"Nobody move," said Bone, softly, as he slowly stepped to the side opposite the creek and drew his .50 caliber handgun to get an angle away from the girls and the wolf-dogs.

He eased the hammer back. The half-cock and full-cock positions made audible sounds heard easily over the bubbling creek and the falls which were only seventy-five yards ahead.

The deadly pit viper turned its triangle-shaped head at the movement and noise from Bone. The pits were easily visible between the eyes and nostrils. Its catlike, elliptical shape pupils gave it an angry, evil look.

There was a slight movement of the head backward as it prepared to strike.

Bone took a good sight picture at the center of its mouth between the two half-inch fangs as his finger tightened on the feather pull trigger. A white blur caused him to instantly relax his finger as Son lunged at the side of the venomous reptile.

He seized it behind the head just as it launched its strike.

"Back up, girls," Bone shouted as Son shook the four foot snake in his jaws like a rat.

Nita and Bear Dog jumped in the fray and each grabbed a portion of the thick-bodied viper. In a matter of seconds, there were three pieces of the reptile lying on the dirt trail—each piece was still wiggling.

Bone stepped in and kicked the heart-shaped head into the creek. "A dead snake can still bite," he told everyone.

He reached down and petted Son, *Nita,* and Bear Dog in turn. "Good job, boys."

Each of the wolf-dogs were wagging their tails as if to say, 'Are we done, now? Huh? Huh?'

Bear Dog had his trademark smile as the front of his lip went up while he wiggled all over.

Jack stepped forward and kicked the rest of the dismembered snake off the trail and gathered the girls in his arms. "Ya'll awright?"

"Uh-huh, Papa," said Aurili Red. "We weren't scared after Son, *Nita*, and Bear Dog pushed us back and got between us that that moccasin."

"I thought snakes would still be denned up," said Silke.

"Warm spell we've had's bringin' some of 'em out. They're real grumpy when they first wake up," said Jack.

"Like someone else I know," commented Angie.

He grinned. "Only till I have a cup of your wonderful coffee, Angiedarlin'."

Bone grabbed Aurali Red and swung her up on his broad shoulders astride his neck as Jack did the same with Baby Sarah. Both girls squealed in delight at riding atop the two men.

"What say we go have some supper, ya'll," said Jack as strode back up the path toward the house.

"Waitin' on me you're backin' up," added Bone from right behind him.

Back at the house, they had all taken their places around the table again. The girls had their own smaller table in the kitchen where they would eat.

Padrino finished telling how he came to be in this time from 2019. "...and I still don't understand how I was able to come to the exact time where Bone and Loraine were with my *moldivite* crystal."

"Amerindians have a sayin' about it, 'If you come to the past, then you are part of the past...and always have been'...Lucy likes it better than their people who just say 'it is written on the great obelisk'," said *Anompoli Lawa*.

"Hope ya'll don't have any more secrets. Just found out about Bone and Loraine comin' from the future and Lucy bein' from another planet just yesterday...an' they even didn't git to the part about Padrino...Gives me a headache."

"Join the club, Riley, I've known 'bout it for over six months an' still ain't got a grasp on it," said Bodie.

"You ain't from the future, are you, Silke?"

She grinned. "Not that I know of, Riley."

"Maybe only yours," muttered Loraine.

Boston turned. "Huh?"

"Nothing," Loraine replied.

Silke turned to Doctor Ashalatubbi as she stabbed a large piece of ham with her fork and placed it in her plate. "Still don't understand why I'm being adopted into the Chickasaw Warriors...I'm a woman."

Winchester sliced his cornbread and put a couple of healthy slabs of butter inside before he answered, "The Chickasaw have a long standing tradition of our women joining the men in battle. Women who wanted to become warriors...became warriors. The Chickasaw *is* a matrilineal society..."

"What does that mean, Doc?" asked Bone.

"It means that ancestral descent is traced through maternal, instead of paternal lines."

"Oh, like a matriarchal society?" asked Loraine.

"Similar, except we have male chiefs...but property belongs to the woman."

"Never knew that," said Bodie.

"As I alluded to earlier, women who participated in battle as strategists and communicators had a clan known as the Panther Women."

Winchester looked around the table and grinned. "Other women would go into battle, singing beautiful songs, which would throw the enemy off guard…and then they would take them out…They were known as the Hatchet Women Clan."

"Which one will I be inducted into?"

His soft brown eyes looked deeply into her sky blue ones. "You shall be of the Hatchet Clan, Silke."

§§§

CHAPTER SEVEN

MCGANN HOME
ARBUCKLE MOUNTAINS

Silke pushed her chair back from the table. "Ooh, ate too much. Think I need to go walk some of this off."

"Me too, that was a wonderful dinner, Angie," said Riley as he, too, pushed away from the table and looked at Silke. "Need some company?"

"Of course, where do you want to walk?"

"Take the path to the falls where the wee *leanaí* were…"

"What's *leanaí*?" asked Loraine.

"Gaelic for babies," answered Angie. "It's back to me first language when it's getting excited I am."

"Just watch out for any more snakes," said Jack.

"Think we're pretty well armed," commented Riley as he patted his .45 Colt.

"Wish I had one of Bone's hand cannons," added Silke.

"I saw that down at the creek…Never seen anythin' like it. What in the world is it?" asked Riley.

"Smith and Wesson .50 caliber 500 model, holds five rounds," answered Bone.

"Oooh-lále…May I?" inquired Boston.

Bone slipped it out of his holster, opened the cylinder, shucked the five large rounds into his hand, and passed the weapon to Riley. "I use a 500 grain round. It will fire up to a 700 grain bullet, but with a lot more recoil…500 will stop just about anything or anybody you need to…just about anywhere you hit 'em."

"Good goshamighty," he said as he hefted the pistol and felt the balance. "See why you called it a hand cannon." He handed it back to Bone.

"You should have seen the hole it put through Big John Tackett," commented Silke as she shook her head again. "Sure wish I had one."

"Won't be making that puppy till 2003," added Bone. He cocked his head in thought and looked at Padrino. "Unless…"

His godfather furrowed his brow and then nodded. "Possible."

"What are ya'll talking about?" asked Loraine.

"Making a round trip to 2019 with Padrino's crystal," said Bone.

"I heard you mention that just before dinner, may I see it?" asked Doctor Ashalatubbi.

Padrino reached in the large side pocket of his cammo BDUs, pulled out the six-inch long, forest green, translucent, teardrop-shaped crystal, and handed it across to Winchester.

The venerable Chickasaw Shaman shivered momentarily when it touched his hand.

"You feel it?" asked Padrino.

"Yes, of course. It was like a rabbit ran across my grave…Like a mild shock…It's warm too." He looked at Padrino. "This is very powerful...Is it emerald?"

Padrino shook his head. "It's a tektite type of crystal, formed from the impact of a giant meteorite...called a *moldavite*. It was given to me by a Navajo Shaman I studied with many long years ago...The old man said it amplifies, channels and expands the power of certain people's spirit energy."

"Yes, I could tell instantly," said *Anompoli Lawa* as he studied the crystal in his hand.

"The Shaman indicated that I was one of these people...You are one also."

"Apparently," replied Ashalatubbi.

"It's not the same as a natural quartz with standard six-sided crystals that grow in a uniform pattern...No forming crystal within the 'mother' crystal of *moldavite* is repeated like a natural crystal would because it doesn't grow...it was formed on a terrific impact...Each and every one of the molecules are different, like snowflakes, because part of it is terrestrial and part is extraterrestrial...That make sense?"

"Oh, absolutely…This is amazing," said Winchester. He looked at Padrino. "Maybe we should try it after Silke's ceremony tomorrow."

Padrino grinned, glanced at Bone and Loraine, and then back at Doctor Ashalatubbi. "I think maybe you're right."

"The two of you?" asked Bone.

"Why not?" replied Padrino. "Let's get the ceremony behind us and then give it a try." He looked back at Winchester. "Game, *Anompoli Lawa*?"

The Shaman smiled and nodded.

"Well, I still need that walk." Silke looked at the Ranger. "Ready Riley?"

He got to his feet and nodded at the door. "After you, m'lady."

The two young people headed to the door.

The three wolf-dogs were asleep under the table after a large meal of their own.

The others exchanged knowing glances and grins after the door closed behind the pair.

"Well, that be a natural paring if I've ever seen one," commented Angie. "It's wondering I am if they know it yet?"

"Time will tell," said *Anompoli Lawa*, with a smile. "No pun intended." He glanced at Padrino.

"Would anyone be needin' more of me coffee?" asked Angie.

Silke and Riley were about ten yards down the path when his hand brushed hers on the narrow trail. Their fingers unconsciously intertwined—or was it unconsciously?

"This is a beautiful area," said Riley as he glanced to their right at the scattered oak, sweet gum, sycamore, pecan, cottonwood, and dogwood trees covering the slope of the rocky hillside, and then back at the crystal clear Honey Creek to their left.

"It is," responded Silke. "Listen."

They focused on the sounds of the forest, cicadas buzzing, squirrels chattering, along with the warble of a killdeer who had just come back north from its winter range in Central America.

They could also hear the mating call of a bright red male cardinal and a mocking bird going through its stolen repertoire—over the gurgle of the creek and the roar of the waterfall eighty yards up the trail around a bend in the creek.

"You could forget all your troubles in a place like this," said Silke. "At least for a little while."

"That's true…Kind of gives you a break to gather your energies for an upcomin' task ahead."

"Oh, look!" She pointed at a mama raccoon leading five little kits across the trail.

"Looks like they're about five weeks old…Mama's probably takin' 'em out on their first outing from the den after birth."

"Betcha she's takin' 'em down to the creek an' gonna show 'em how to find mussels."

The mama noticed the pair approaching and churred to her babies to hurry up as she led them into the woods between the trail and the creek.

Silke and Riley rounded the turn in the trail and could finally see the falls tumbling down the travertine shelves and rocks to the large pool at the bottom. The water was over fifteen feet deep around and out from the base

There was a huge boulder out about fifteen feet from the bottom of the falls that had apparently fallen from the cliff many years earlier.

"Oh, isn't that a cave behind the falls?" asked Silke.

"Looks like it," answered Riley. "A person could stand up in there...interesting."

"Over there are three wickiups." Silke looked to the right of the falls. "Must be for the ceremony...Two big ones an' a small one. Wonder how they fit in?"

"Reckon you'll find out in the mornin'.

Riley turned to face Silke. "Has anyone ever told you that you have the most amazin' blue eyes?"

She blushed and looked away across the wide pool. "Not really."

"Feller could get lost in there...they're so deep."

She glanced back up at him. "Yours aren't too bad either...They kinda scare me, a little."

Riley frowned and furrowed his brow. "How do you mean?"

"They, uh...look like they're peerin' into my very soul."

"Well, if they are...They like what they see."

She cleared her throat and looked up at the sun as the edge of the disk disappeared behind the top of the falls, sending millions of sparkling red, yellow, and silver diamonds reflecting off the churning water coming down the mountain side.

"Uh…Guess we should start back, it will be dark soon."

"Yeah, don't want to step on another one of those moccasins in the shadows," he replied.

Silke nodded and they headed back to the path, still hand-in-hand.

Silke and Riley climbed the steps to the porch where everyone else was sitting enjoying after dinner coffee and the sunset.

"It was being concerned we were ye weren't goin' to be back before the gloamin'," commented Angie.

"The time sorta slipped away from us, it was so beautiful down there at the falls," said Silke.

"We saw the cave behind the falls, too. Looked haunted," added Riley.

Jack, Angie, and *Anompoli Lawa* exchanged glances.

"It is," replied Jack.

"Really?" asked Silke.

"Back before I met my beautiful Angie, I was doin' some undercover work with Chickasaw Lighthorse Montford Anoatubbi, as gold prospectors. There was a small gold rush goin' on at the time an' there were some claim jumpers we were after…"

"Me sweet Jack an' Montford were attacked by the brigands. They killed poor Montford an' wounded me Jack an' him fallin' into the creek which was up to white water stage from a heavy rain," Angie interrupted.

"I was washed, mostly unconscious, down the rapids an' over the falls, just missin that big rock at the bottom…"

"Somehow it was he managed to swim over to the falls an' clamber up behind it into the cave. It was Son's daddy, Boy, he had with him who had followed him as he was washed down the mountain," Angie interrupted.

"Boy laid down beside me, with me bein' unconscious from one of the claim jumper's bullets bouncin' off my noggin'…Saved my life, he did."

Jack glanced over at Angie. "Then, next thing I know, this little eight year old girl with corn silk hair was squattin' down beside me. I asked who she was an' she said her name was Anna an' what was mine an' I didn't know…reckon I passed out again, then."

"Boy came an' scratched at me door an' made me follow him back to the cave, he did…It was tending to Jack I was, when he woke up an' said I'd growed a mite and then he passed out again. I left to get me medicines and blankets…"

"Guess I woke up again an' that little girl was back an' I said, 'Wish you'd make up yer mind…'Er you gonna be big or little and why are there two of ya?'…an' she said she brought my hat an' guns, but, had to go an' disappeared around the edge of the falls. Then Angie come back in with all her fixin's…"

She interrupted him again. "Faith and what in the world I asked meself as beside him all his guns and hat were layin', and his eyes opened and he squinted up at meself for a moment and said, 'Wish you'd make up yer mind,'…I asked him what is it he meant?"

"I remember this part. I asked her if she was gonna be big 'er…little?" said Jack.

"It was daft he was…out of his head, I thought…Then he asked how I got there and I told him his dog came and got me, but he dinna like Shakespeare."

Jack chuckled. "Boy likes Keats…I read to him from a book of his poetry."

Everyone exchanged glances and grinned.

"Then he told me about the little girl with the corn silk hair who was in earlier, once he figured out we weren't the same," said Angie.

"I told her the little girl said her name was Anna."

Angie looked at everyone on the porch, including her smiling and nodding uncle as he listened to the story.

Her eyes filled with tears when she took a breath and said with her voice breaking, "Anna was me daughter…She drowned in that pool when she fell in the creek above the falls…three years before while she was pickin' jonquils…We had never found her wee sweet body."

§§§

CHAPTER EIGHT

DEXTER HOTEL
DEXTER, TEXAS

"You get the boys set up to meet us at Caddo?" Duce asked Goose as they stepped out of the front of the hotel and headed down the boardwalk to the Sugar Hill Saloon for supper.

Merkins glanced at Walton out of the corner of his eye. "Said to, didn't ya?"

"Jest checkin'. Don't aim to git my ass in a crack on account of somethin' not workin' as planned. How many you git rounded up?"

"Seven…Logan brothers an' their cousins."

Duce nodded. "Good…They're a tight bunch an' foller orders."

"Mazeppa's bringin' his dynamite gear…iff'n the express agent don't want to cooperate."

"Hope we don't have to use it. Last time he overdid it an' burnt up or scattered most of the money to hell an' gone."

Goose pushed opened the tall doors, and then the batwings to allow the two outlaws to enter the dimly lit saloon. The air inside was a smoky haze and smelled of stale beer, tobacco smoke, and urine.

The owner and bartender, Ed Stein, looked up from drying a four ounce gill glass at the sound of the doors closing. "Evenin' boys, what'll it be?"

"What's fer supper, Ed?" asked Duce.

"Got cat's ass an' cabbage tonight."

"Funny man," said Goose.

"Naw, got my special Red River venison chili…It'll make yer hair sweat."

"Sounds good. Needin' to clean out my plumbin' anyways," commented Duce.

"Shore glad we got separate rooms," mumbled Goose.

"What's that?" asked Duce.

"Oh...Uh, said gonna be a gibbous moon tonight."

Duce frowned and squinted his eyes at the slim man.

MCGANN HOME
ARBUCKLE MOUNTAINS

"Well, here she comes," said Jack as they watched the three-quarter gibbous moon peek over the tree-covered ridge line on the east side of Honey Creek, casting her silvery beams through the barren limbs of the winter-killed trees hanging over the water way down below the log house.

The pleasant sounds of crickets, frogs, and night owls filled the air as Angie walked around with her big blue graniteware coffee pot, filling her guests cups out on the wide porch.

"It's going inside and putting the girls to bed, I am...My wee babies are wanting me to read the rest of a book Aurali Red brought with her, *Alice's*

Adventures in Wonderland...Faith and it's a wonder they don't know it by heart...this being the third time I've read it to them."

"And twice for me, Angiedarlin'," added Jack.

"Long as they're being read to," said Doctor Ashalatubbi.

Angie nodded. "Aye, it tis, Uncle," she said as she went back inside.

"Where do you recommend we go to try to activate an electromagnetic vortex after Silke's ceremony, *Anompoli Lawa*?" asked Padrino.

The venerable Shaman smiled. "We won't have to go far, I don't think."

"How so?" asked Bone.

He glanced over at the big man. "That cave Jack crawled up into behind the falls..."

"Don't tell me there are petroglyphs in there and one of them is a..."

"Correct, Padrino. One of them is an open spiral...carved next to a *Menorah*."

"Are you talkin' about the seven-lamp Hebrew lampstand Moses used in the exodus?" asked Silke.

"And later in the Temple at Jerusalem," added Padrino.

Doctor Ashalatubbi nodded. "All the carvings in the cave preceded the arrival of even the *Atakapan Tejas* Indian tribe...part of the *Caddos*...over a thousand years ago. Most likely at least Neolithic."

"How could the *Menorah* be carved in a cave in North America long before Columbus?" asked Loraine.

Winchester looked around the porch. "I'm sure you've all heard of the lost tribes of Israel?"

There were nods from all.

"Some say there were ten...others, that there were twelve. Now, what I'm about to tell, you can make up your own mind about...The Cherokee elders call their ancestors...the *AniKituwahYah* and they referred to the Great Spirit as *YoHeWaH*."

"Hey, that sounds like..."

Anompoli Lawa interrupted Bone, "*Yahweh*...Yes, one of the names in the *Torah* for God, along with *Jehovah* and *Elohim*...among others...The Choctaw have a legend of how the Great Spirit came to a man called *Nuah*...and told him to build a great raft to save mankind because the world would soon be covered with water."

"Ooh, this is almost as heavy as all ya'll bein' from the future and your friend Lucy from another

91

planet," said Riley as he looked at Bone, Loraine, and Padrino.

"Oh, there's more. One of the Chickasaw words for God is *Chí-hóo-wah*…and a common expression we have when someone is leaving is…*Chí-hóo-wah-bia-chi*…Go with God."

Padrino nodded. "Sounds awfully close to *Jehovah*…I would say with the open spiral being inside that cave along with the depiction of the *Menorah*, is good enough for me to try a shot." He looked at his watch. "Let's see if the girls are at the ranch near the statue."

He pulled his Galaxy S9. "Uh-oh, battery getting low. I put it in the wrong pocket."

"What do you mean?" asked Silke.

"I've found that if I keep it in the same pocket with the *moldavite* crystal, it keeps a charge," answered Padrino.

"Those things amaze me," said Bodie. "I even got to talk to those girls in the future he just mentioned when we were after that gold down in the Brazos." He glanced at Silke and Riley. "They're both law officers in Bone an' thems time."

"Use my S7, Padrino," said Bone. "It's got a full charge from that ruby thing Lucy put in it in 2014." He handed his smart phone over.

Padrino nodded, put the phone on speaker, held it against the crystal, and hit Peach's speed dial. One ring, two rings, three.

"Bone, Bone, Bone," screamed the Forensics Technician, Peach Presley, through the speaker, "It's you!"

"No, its Padrino, Peach, but Bone, Loraine, Bodie, Silke Justice, Texas Ranger Riley Boston, Marshal Jack McGann, and *Anompoli Lawa* are all here with me up at Turner Falls."

"Bless your hearts, ya'll havin' a charivari?"

"Not quite, Peach…"

BONE'S RANCH 2019

"Hold your taters, gotta get Stella. She's doin' somethin' to her hair in the bathroom. Girl will have a hissy fit she doesn't get to talk to ya'll…Stella! Stella! Get your bubble-butt in here…It's Bone an' them."

The drop-dead gorgeous blond Inspector from the Gainesville Police Department came running into the kitchen where Peach had been sitting having a slice of apple pie.

Her boat-neck T-shirt was pulled down around her shoulders while she was touching up the lighter streaks in her long tresses.

"Law, Buttercup pull that up! We kin see clear to the promised land!"

"We're not on face-time are we?" she said as she pulled the T back up.

"No, but that's a good idea." Peach keyed her video and squealed, "It works...This just dills my pickle..."

MCGANN HOME
ARBUCLKE MOUNTAINS 1899

Bone reached over and hit his video button. A close-up picture of a brunette Peach and a blond Stella crowded the screen. Big grins were across their faces.

"Lord love a duck," Bone said. "Peach, hold the phone arms length away, we can count the nose hairs."

"Damn you, Bone, I'm gonna kill you...Sometimes you just make my ass itch," said Peach as she held the phone out away from her and Stella.

Silke glanced at Loraine, grinned, and mouthed, "I like them."

"Good people. Smart as whips," mouthed Loraine back.

"Listen, ladies, need ya'll to do something," said Padrino.

"You name it, Honey Bear," answered Peach.

"Need you and Stella to get Bone's spare Smith & Wesson 500 and come up to Turner Falls."

"Do what? His 500? Turner Falls?...Well, where in the world is that dang hand cannon?" asked Peach.

"My go bag, top shelf, my closet...Hell just bring the whole bag," said Bone.

"Sure, but what's at Turner Falls?" asked Stella.

"*Anompoli Lawa* and me," said Padrino. "Tomorrow about noon."

"Oh, my, I'm gonna get the vapors," said Peach.

"Chickasaw Shaman, *Anompoli Lawa*, thinks there's another portal at the falls," commented Bone.

Peach and Stella exchanged grins. "Bless ya'lls hearts, funny you should mention that. Been doin' some research on magnetic ley lines…You know, Padrino, you said that portal at Possum Kingdom was probably on one."

"Yeah, and?" asked Padrino.

"Just so happens, sweet pea, there is a ley line runnin' from the great lakes all the way down to Acapulco, Mexico…" Peach's grin got even bigger. "and just so happens it goes through the Arbuckles, Gainesville, and Possum Kingdom…Now, ain't that finer than a frog hair split four ways?"

"What's a magnetic ley line?" asked Silke.

Padrino looked over at her. "It's an electromagnetic fault line in the tectonic crust."

Her blue eyes kind of glazed over. "Right."

"Don't forget…tomorrow noon, ladies…"

Bone's screen went dark.

"Ladies?…Gone." Padrino looked over at Doctor Ashalatubbi. "Well, there you have it."

"Amazing, simply amazing," he replied shaking his head.

A stunned Riley shook his head also. "Think I need to go to my bedroll. Got a lot to process here."

"It's somethin' new most every time I'm around ya'll," said Silke.

"You gotta admit, girl, we do keep things interesting," said Bone with his enigmatic grin.

"Riley has a good idea." Winchester looked at Silke. "Speaking of interesting, I think you're going to find tomorrow will fit in that category nicely...Best get some rest and be prepared."

"Believe you're right," Silke said as she pushed to her feet and headed to the front door.

Everyone, but Winchester, followed her lead.

"Think I'll sit out here a little while longer and enjoy the evening," he said.

The mournful howl of a wolf pierced the quiet. Son, *Nita*, and Bear Dog all got to their feet and looked over toward a ridge just under the rising moon. A silhouette of a wolf, his nose raised to the sky in another howl, was atop a rock outcrop.

"Son's daddy, Boy," said Jack before he turned and went inside.

§§§

CHAPTER NINE

MCGANN HOME
ARBUCKLE MOUNTAINS

Jack and Angie's big Rhode Island Red rooster with long black tail feathers welcomed the morning sun, even though it hadn't quite broken the horizon.

Red and gold arrows streaked across the sky from the pink glow, chasing the purple and black night to the west.

The rooster was perched on the top rail of the paddock next to the barn on the east side of the house. He crowed again and fluffed his wings with his self-imposed importance of announcing the coming day.

The horses in the corral were all standing at the fence, staring, and nickering at the house, awaiting their morning allotment of grain and flakes of alfalfa.

The three-quarter moon had tracked to about twenty degrees above the western horizon, its light weakly competing with the glow on the eastern side as the day promised to be an abnormally warm one, even for spring.

Bodie opened one eye and looked out the screen from his soogan at the corral. "Damn rooster," he mumbled and started to roll over when he smelled the fragrance of coffee from the open door to the kitchen.

He sat up to see Doctor Ashalatubbi coming up the outside steps to the screen door from the privy over near the tree line.

"Going to sleep all day, gentlemen?" he said as he came inside and let the screen door slam shut with a bang.

Riley shot up and glanced around with confusion and then spied Winchester's back disappearing into the kitchen.

He and Bodie saw Padrino's bedroll was empty and looked at each other.

"Guess everybody's in the kitchen havin' coffee," commented Bodie.

"Smells good," Riley replied. "Gotta see a man about a dog, then I'll join you." He reached over and grabbed his boots, shook them to dislodge any boarders and pulled them on.

Bodie joined him at the screen door after going through the same routine. "Gotta see the same feller."

They both headed out at a fast walk toward the privy or the woods behind it.

Angie was mixing pancake batter in a large bowl while everyone, but Bodie and Riley, was having coffee at the large round breakfast table in the big kitchen.

The aroma of hot coffee and sizzling bacon on the stove permeated the room.

"Does anything smell better in the morning than coffee and bacon cooking?" commented Bone as he took a sip of his coffee from a white ceramic cup.

"Just wait till my Angiedarlin starts dippin' dollops of her buttermilk pancakes on that hot griddle," said Jack.

Bodie and Riley came through the side door from the porch.

"Hope there's some coffee left," said Bodie.

"We're on the second pot," answered Loraine.

Silke glanced over at Doctor Ashalatubbi. "What time are you going to start the ceremony?"

"I suspect about eight o'clock, child, just about sunup. The women are already down at the falls making the preparations."

"How do you know that, Doc?" asked Bone.

"Heard them go by about five," he replied. "They had to get the fire started for the sweat lodge."

Jack grinned as he filled Bodie and Riley's cups. "You're gonna love that, Silke."

"For some reason, that sounds ominous," she replied as she raked several slices of bacon in her plate as Angie gave her the first three pancakes.

They all looked up as Red Wolf entered from the porch. "*Shee-ah*."

"*Shee-ah*, Red Wolf, replied *Anompoli Lawa*.

Everyone else passed the traditional greeting to the Chickasaw Lighthorse.

"Like some coffee, Red Wolf?" asked Angie.

"Uhhh, me like."

Angie poured him a cup and set it on the table. "Do your own fixin'."

He picked up a spoon and ladled his usual five teaspoons of sugar into his cup and gave it a quick stir.

Thirty minutes later, everyone had finished their breakfast. Aurali Red and Baby Sarah sat at their little table with steaming bowls of oatmeal in front of them. Both were trying to rub the sleep from their eyes.

Winchester turned to Silke. "My dear, I suggest we head on down to the falls, the ladies will have to make you ready."

"Do I need to take anything?" she asked.

Anompoli Lawa looked at her a moment and then replied as he got to his feet, "I think not." He turned to the others. "Ya'll can come down in an hour…after the cleansing has been done."

Silke snapped a look at the Shaman. "Cleansin'?"

He nodded and motioned to the door. "Come along, child."

It only took Silke and *Anompoli Lawa* a few minutes to walk the one hundred yards down the trail to the falls.

There were five Chickasaw women in traditional Regalia dress, white doeskin wraparound skirts and colorful beaded ribbon shirts. They wore Chickasaw style beaded moccasins where the seam was on the top and a two inch flap turned down at the ankle.

Anompoli Lawa disappeared inside one of the two large wickiups with two of the women.

The other three women took Silke by the hand and led her inside the other large wickiup, closing the deerskin flap behind them.

They started to undress Silke. At first she was confused and resisted, but one of the women shook her head. She relented and the women removed her clothing, leaving her standing in the middle of the wickiup, stark naked.

They took coarse muslin cloths, dipped them into a bowl of warm water with an aromatic odor of lilac and balsam and scrubbed her body.

Each of the women picked up short fresh cedar branches from a pile at the side of the wickiup in each hand after drying her off. They rhythmically began to dance around Silke, chanting and thrashing her body all over lightly with the boughs.

Even with the light touch, the green cedar stung her skin, but she was determined to show no discomfort and stood motionless.

The thrashing continued for almost five minutes until her skin fairly glowed a bright pink.

The women stopped, laid down their cedar boughs, and picked up earthenware bowls containing a thick brown liquid. They started spreading the liquid over her trim body, rubbing it in well with their bare hands.

She could discern the odor of cinnamon and cloves with a touch of peppermint or wintergreen, and her skin started tingling as the women applied the mixture with a gentle touch—even to her hair.

They re-braided it, wrapped the bottom third with a white doeskin band, and then slipped a beaded headband around her brow. One of the women wrapped her well-shaped breasts with a butter-soft, white beaded doeskin halter while another wound a skirt of identical beaded white doeskin around her hips where it fell just past her knees. The third woman slipped matching white moccasins on her tiny feet.

The three women stood back, appraised their work, nodded to each other and ushered Silke back outside.

Everyone, but Angie, who stayed to mind the girls and keep the wolfdogs inside, had come down from the house. They were standing together, a respectful distance from the liturgical area along with a number of ceremonial clad Chickasaw men and women warriors.

Riley's chin hit his chest when he saw Silke's well-shaped, perfectly proportioned body.

"My God, an Aphrodite," he muttered.

Bodie elbowed him in the side.

Anompoli Lawa exited the other wickiup. He was dressed in a white beaded warshirt, matching leggings, breechclout, moccasins, and a beaded headband with three eagle feathers in the back, pointed down. His face was painted in red ocher with blue around his eyes.

He carried his personal totem carved from a piece of lightning-riven hickory and a decorated gourd rattle. The Shaman stuck the rattle in his belt, reached into a beaded medicine bag hung around his neck and pulled out a small pouch. He opened it, took a pinch of sacred dogwood pollen and scattered some to each of the four directions. Then he took another pinch and sprinkled it over Silke's head.

The men and women warriors, all in ceremonial battle dress and with weapons, began a rhythmic dance around the pair to the beat of rawhide drums by two of the women who had prepared Silke.

The Shaman also danced in a reverse circle around her, creating a circle within a circle, shaking his rattle, waving his totem about her and chanting.

The dance continued until *Anompoli Lawa* raised his totem in the air and the women on the drums stopped.

He motioned to the warriors to set the smaller hide-covered wickiup over the hickory and pecan wood fire which had burned down to glowing hot coals.

One of the warriors put a large earthen pot of blessed water with a gourd dipper inside next to the hot granite stream-tumbled rocks around the coals. Each rock was about the size of a cantaloupe. Next to the water pot was a small bowl of a thick brownish liquid.

The women had placed tanned deerskins on either side of the ring of rocks.

Another of the women warriors entered the lodge with a smoking sage wand to purify the air inside and ward off evil spirits.

The Shaman nodded to Silke to enter through the deerskin flap covering the entrance as the female warrior exited.

They sat cross-legged on the hides across the red-hot bed of coals from each other in the semi darkness.

Anompoli Lawa handed her the small bowl. "Drink half of this.

Silke smelled of the contents and wrinkled her nose. "Oh, my Lord, what is this?"

"Don't ask, just drink it quickly. It will help put you in a meditative state. She drank half of the pungent liquid, almost gagged, but kept it down, and handed the bowl back to him.

He drank the balance, set the bowl down, and then poured three dippers of the holy water on the hot rocks. They hissed and popped as steam boiled upwards and rapidly filled the small dome.

Silke could feel the heat emanating from the ages old granite rocks. An ethereal glow—different from the red hot coals—and without any obvious source—slowly brightened the thick cloud of swirling steam.

Colored lights began to swirl about and pulsate to the same rhythm as their heartbeats.

After a moment, the Shaman repeated the process as the rocks heated back up. The moist heat was stifling. Silke was having trouble breathing—then there was a bright light.

Silke could feel herself rise out of her body and float in the white steam cloud—she could no longer feel the heat. There was no up or down. Her body was pure spirit. She looked down at herself sitting across from *Anompoli Lawa*.

Images began to swirl about—battle images. They faded and she could see herself in a gunfight with a band of outlaws. She had Bone's big gun in one hand and a tomahawk in the other.

One of the men on her left aimed at Riley. She only had time to sling the tomahawk at him with her left hand just as he fired. She saw someone fall in the smoke. Then the battle faded away.

A beautiful Chickasaw woman in a white beaded doeskin full length dress approached out of the steam. She held up her hand. "I am *Te Ata*...Bearer of the Dawn. I come from the future. You will become a great warrior, hereafter known to the Chickasaw as *Kowishto' Ihoo Hommá* - Red Hair Woman...There will be death..."

The image faded as the steam began to disappear.

"No! Please wait. Don't go...Who..."

"It is too late, we shall receive no more," said *Anompoli Lawa* as he nodded toward the doorway.

She crawled out past the flap, followed by *Anompoli Lawa*. As soon as they were both outside, the five women who had prepared her, doused them both with buckets of ice cold water from all sides.

Silke screamed. "Oh, my sweet Jesus! That's freezing! What was that for?" she asked, shivering.

The white-haired Shaman wrapped his arms about his bony chest, also shivering. "To cleanse our souls, my child, and bring us back to reality."

Two of the warrior women wrapped blankets around the freezing people.

The five women set their buckets down and led Silke back over to the first wickiup and took her inside.

Anompoli Lawa re-entered his.

In ten minutes, they each came back out. Silke was dressed in her new custom doeskins that did nothing to hide her shapely figure. They were decorated in Chickasaw beadwork. Her hair had been brushed out and rebraided.

Winchester walked up to her in a full set of beaded buckskins and held out a Chickasaw war tomahawk—decorated with brass brads around the hickory handle—with both hands.

"You have completed the right of warrior passage, as a Hatchet Woman, signifying female leadership and strength in the Chickasaw Nation Wolf Clan. *Ababinili-hoyo-aboha-ona, Kowishto'*

Ihoo Hommá Chihóa-bia-chee...May the Great Spirit guide you, Red Hair Woman...Go with God."

The other Chickasaw warriors repeated, "*Chihoa-bia-chee, Kowishto' Ihoo Hommá.*"

Anompoli Lawa hung a small talisman of crossed tomahawks made of hammered silver on a leather thong around her neck.

She looked down at the necklace and admired the workmanship of the warhawks.

Bone, Loraine, and the others stepped forward to congratulate her as she slipped the warhawk in her beaded belt on her right side in front of her Bowie.

"Well, how do you feel, Silke?" asked Padrino.

She pursed her lips, looked first at him, and then the others with apprehension in her cerulean blue eyes. "Someone is going to die."

§§§

CHAPTER TEN

TURNER FALLS, IT

"What happened in there, Silke?" asked Loraine.

She shook her head and took a breath. "Not completely sure. Saw a lot of things...colors and all."

"We could hear you talking to someone," said Bone.

Silke nodded. "A Chickasaw woman named *Te Ata*. Said she was from the future…"

Anompoli Lawa pointed to a four year old child standing next to her mother in the crowd of Chickasaw watching. "That's her over there…She was born in 1895."

"Well, heard of her…in our time. She died in 1995 at age 100. *Te Ata* was a great stage actress and storyteller. Even performed for FDR…"

"Who's FDR?" asked Bodie.

"Franklin Delano Roosevelt, President of the United States from 1933 to 1945."

"Related to Teddy?" asked Bodie.

"Cousins," replied Padrino. "Anyway, she performed at the White House and for the crown heads of Europe…Famous lady."

"What did she say?" asked Riley.

"Mostly that I would become a great warrior…but that there would be death."

"Say who?" asked Loraine.

Silke shook her head. "I took her to mean someone that I know."

They all exchanged glances.

"It is what it is," said Bone. "What will be, will be."

Silke looked up at the sun in surprise. "It's nearly noon!"

"Yeah, ya'll were in that sweatlodge for quite a while," replied Jack.

"It seemed like only minutes," she replied.

Doctor Ashalatubbi glanced over at Padrino. "Perhaps we should get ready for our sojourn."

Padrino nodded. "I think so."

Winchester motioned to two of the preparation ladies to bring the deerskins he and Silke sat on inside the sweatlodge.

The women brought them forward and handed them to the doctor and Padrino.

They looked at the others and Padrino handed the blue enigma crystal to Bone. "Here, just in case we can't get back...You should be able to communicate with 2019 with this power crystal that Lenny had...But, hope we're back in a bit."

He and the Shaman turned and headed to the falls. In a few minutes, they disappeared down the path behind the roaring water.

Silke glanced at Bone and Loraine. "This should be interesting."

GAINESVILLE PD - 2019

"How about I go with ya'll?" suggested Captain St. John. "Never ridden in Bone's Cord."

"Sure, might as well," answered Stella.

"Bone said to drive it once in a while, anyway...bless his little ol' pea pickin' heart," said Peach.

The trio walked out of the Gainesville PD, across the street to the police parking lot and approached Bone's pristine sky blue, 1930 L-29 Cord Coupe. The top was down since it was a nice spring day.

Lucy had signed the antique automobile—the first front wheel drive made in America—over to Bone when she was rescued by her people in 2014.

The rare car was in addition to the house and section of land she had inherited from Sheriff Mason Flynn's sister, Mary Lou and her husband, Cletus Wilson, when they passed away in the Spanish flu pandemic of 1918. The deadly flu killed over 50 million people world wide, with some 675,000 in America.

"Any chance I could drive it?" asked the stocky, bald, black, Chief of Police.

Stella and Peach exchanged glances.

"Don't see why not, Cap'n, you've known him longer than we have," answered Stella. "I'll just pass along what he said, 'Don't hurt it'."

He grinned. "I won't...Yeah, doesn't seem possible I was his commanding officer in the Marine Corps, then get him in my police department...and still haven't killed him."

Peach giggled. "Oh, ya'll are just like brothers, fuss an' fight, but still do anythin' for each other...Ya'll couldn't buy a hummin'bird on a string for a nickel."

St. John stopped at the driver's door of the Cord and looked at his Forensics Tech from Georgia. "Peach, what the hell does that mean?"

She giggled again. "Honey, sure as cornbread goes with turnip greens. I don't have a clue, it was just somethin' my granny always said."

St. John shook his head, got in, turned the key, and stepped on the starter button bringing the big Lycoming inline eight cylinder engine roaring to life.

"Dang that's pretty," he said as he listened to it purr.

"Wait'll you hit the gas," said Stella as she got in the small back seat.

"Oh, boy." He put the floor shift in reverse, backed out of the parking slot, put it in first, and pulled out onto the street.

They turned west on Summit Street, drove the three blocks to I-35, got onto the northbound ramp and merged into the sparse traffic.

"'Bout an hour to Turner Falls?" St. John asked.

"If you drive the speed limit, sweet pea...Uh, Cap'n," said Peach from the passenger's seat.

He looked at the attractive brunette from the corner of his eye, shifted into third, and accelerated toward the Red River, only seven miles away.

TURNER FALLS - 1899

The two men spread their deerskins, side by side, on the floor of the dank cave. Padrino pulled out his tac light and shined it across to the north wall on the petroglyphs.

117

"My, my, that's amazing," he said as he panned the powerful light across the ancient carvings. "That spiral is identical to the one in the cave down on the Brazos we came through...You could almost say the same person carved them."

"Could be," said *Anompoli Lawa*, with a grin.

Padrino pulled the *moldavite* crystal from the large BDU side pocket and sat down cross-legged on one of skins.

Anompoli Lawa sat on the other, directly in front of Padrino—their knees almost touched.

"I do the Zen type of meditation," said Padrino.

"As do I...Studied it extensively when I was in medical college," said the Shaman.

Padrino laid the six inch long light green crystal across both his palms and extended them out towards Winchester. The Shaman placed his hands, palm down, on top of the crystal, their fingertips and the heels of their hands touched, creating a pocket.

Both men closed their eyes and regulated their breathing—slow, deep and rhythmic.

Soon, their breath synchronized and became very soft, even slower, and shallow like in deep

REM sleep—enhanced by the white sound of the water pouring past the entrance.

A pale green glow leaked out between their hands and fingers, and got stronger the deeper the two shamanistic men went into the Zen state.

The glow permeated the dark recesses of the ancient cave and seemed to pulse for a long moment at the same rhythm as their heartbeats, and then it slowly subsided.

Anompoli Lawa was the first to open his eyes and Padrino followed shortly thereafter. The two men blinked several times and looked around the interior of the cave, and then at the water rushing by the opening.

"Looks the same," said Padrino.

"Most likely it would. I suppose we'll know when we go back outside."

"Wait." Padrino pulled his phone out and looked at the face. "Ha! Got bars." He showed it to Winchester.

"And that means what?"

"That at least we're in a time where there are cell phone towers broadcasting a signal."

TURNER FALLS PARK - 2019

St. John turned off I-35 at exit #47 onto old hwy. 77. They drove around hairpin curves until they came to the Turner Falls Park entrance. They stopped at the gate house.

"Be ten dollars and fifty cents. That's three-fifty each," said the attendant.

St. John flashed his badge, hoping the woman inside wouldn't notice it was from Gainesville, Texas. "Police officers."

The middle-aged woman leaned forward on her elbows toward her small window opening on the drive through. "Mister, I don't care if you're the governor himself, it's three-fifty apiece until it's summer time, you want to come in the park." She bobbed her head one time and leaned back.

The captain frowned and started to reach for his billfold when Stella handed him a ten dollar bill and a fifty cent piece from the back seat.

He passed the money on to the dour attendant and waited until she raised the bar blocking the road.

"You can park over there in those lots." She indicated the parking areas on both sides of the road. "Or there are probably some spots in the lots on the right side before you get to the rock castles…an' just so you know, the water's still a mite cold for swimmin'…but up to you."

St. John nodded. "Thank you." He put the Cord in gear and pulled through the entry.

"Why don't you pull in over there at Onion Burgers and let's get some lunch. If Padrino and that Shaman he mentioned made it through, they might be hungry," said Stella.

"I'm so hungry I could eat the north end of a southbound goat," added Peach.

The captain pulled up next to the burger building.

"I'll get 'em," said Peach. "Everbody want mustard, lettuce, tomato, pickles, an' onions on your cheeseburgers?"

"Mayo for me, and no pickles," said St. John.

Peach looked back at him, raised her eyebrow as she turned around and muttered under her breath, "Damn yankee."

Padrino and *Anompoli Lawa* started over to the path leading out from behind the falls.

Padrino stopped. "Oops, if we did make it to 2019, better put this .45 in my BDU pocket. You wouldn't believe the panic it might cause, plus we'd be in Oklahoma and I don't have a carry license for this state."

He unclipped the paddle holster from his combat belt and slipped it in the opposite thigh pocket from where his smart phone and the *moldavite* crystal were.

"So we become a state?" questioned Winchester.

"Yep, 1907…they combined the Nations and Oklahoma Territory and Oklahoma became the twenty-first state in the union."

He followed the Shaman out the narrow ledge to the outside and over to the sandy bank.

Anompoli Lawa glanced around at some of the people who were laying on beach towels warming in the midday sun. His eyes focused on the amount of soft drink cans and other trash over the area.

"This is sacrilege," he mumbled.

Padrino nodded. "Yep, we're in our time. Seems like many of the folks coming for an outing to these type places have little to no respect for the land or the environment."

Winchester looked over to the south side of the large pool at the base of the falls. "What's that?"

"I'd say it looks like bath houses and rest rooms...privys," answered Padrino.

"Well, at least they don't use the woods."

Padrino frowned. "Wouldn't count on that, either."

The doctor's eyes took in the rest of the area and saw the concrete walkway and retaining wall that went across the east end of the pond and Honey Creek to the south side.

He shook his head. "They've destroyed the aesthetics of the area. Such a pity...I think I see why you like our time."

The retired Marine nodded. "This all belongs to the state now. They turned it into a park and you can see the result."

"Brings tears to my eyes. They have raped our land," replied the elder Shaman as he looked around and shook his head.

Padrino looked up at the trail that followed the creek as it curved to the north and saw Captain St. John, Stella, and Peach, walking in their direction.

"Looky there...grinnin' like a possum eatin' a sweet tater," said Peach as she waved at Padrino and *Anompoli Lawa* with her left hand—her right carried a white paper sack.

Stella carried Bone's brown leather go-bag.

§§§

CHAPTER ELEVEN

CADDO, IT

The big black 4x4x2 KATY locomotive eased forward, blowing steam from her relief valves as she did, to center the tender under the waterspout of the tank.

The colored fireman crawled atop the tender, grabbed the chain, and pulled the metal spout down, inserting the canvas sleeve into the open hatch. The gushing water would have the reservoir filled in a matter of minutes.

That was just enough time for Amos Logan to run from his hiding place, clamber up into the engineer's cab, and stick his gun in the man's ribs.

"Jest keep yer hand off'n that Johnson bar jackanape, we'll be a lettin' you go in jest a little bit."

The six other men from Logan's gang galloped out of the trees, thirty yards to the east of the track. One of the men led Amos's horse and another led two more.

Duce Walton and his partner, Goose Merkins, stepped down the steel steps from the passenger car behind the express car. Both were garishly dressed as drummers.

One of the tobymen pointed his gun at the fireman on top of the tender. "You jest sit down right there, nigger, when you finish fillin' yer tank an' don't move till we be done…Hear?"

"Yassa, I hears ya…I be rightchere."

He pulled the chain up, lifting the end of the spout from the tank hatch, letting the counter weight carry it back up to the ready position—then he sat down and rolled himself a smoke.

Walton and Goose stepped up to the big sliding door of the express car to join Mazeppa Logan and the others already waiting alongside.

"Mazeppa, send a couple of the boys back along the train while we take care of this," said Walton.

"Dog, you an' Herky go relieve the passengers of their valuables, keep 'em inside an' take care of any heroes," said Logan.

The two outlaws nodded, dismounted, handed their reins to one of the other cousins, and went back to the passenger cars.

Goose Merkins stepped up to the express car door and rapped on it with butt of his Colt. "Open up in there an' stand an' deliver...You hearin' me?"

A muffled shaky voice came from inside, "I hear you and no, sir, I cain't open the door."

"Now, feller, yer bein' dumber than a bucket of rocks," answered Goose.

"I work for the KATY railroad an' am responsible for everything in this car."

"Who's responsible fer you livin' er dyin'?" asked Duce.

"Uh...Reckon I am."

"What's yer name?" Duce continued.

"Charles…Charles W. Haas…Sir."

"Got a family, Charlie?"

"Uh…Yessir, wife an' a little girl."

"What's their names?"

"Sarah's my wife an' Lizbeth's my daughter."

"Who' responsible fer them?" Duce continued.

"Guess I am," replied Haas.

"Know what dynamite is, Charlie?"

"Uh…Yessir, reckon I do."

"Know what will happen if'n we put three er four sticks underneath this here car, Charlie?"

There was a moment of silence, then several clicks, and the sound of a steel bolt being pulled back. The big sliding door opened three feet and two double barreled shotguns sailed out of the car to the ground.

A slight built, balding man wearing a green visor and wire-rimmed glasses, and two nervous blue uniformed guards stood just inside the door with their hands in the air.

"Smart move, Charlie," said Duce as he and Merkins clambered up into the car. "Now open that damn safe." He looked back at Mazeppa and nodded…

TURNER FALLS, 2019

"Oh, Padrino, I'm just gonna hug the stuffin' out of you," said Peach.

She wrapped her arms around the elderly man, hugged him and pecked him on the lips.

"Hey, Peach." He hugged her back and looked over at Stella and St. John. "Stella, Cap'n...Want ya'll to meet Doctor Winchester Ashalatubbi, he's also the shaman for the Chickasaw Nation. His tribal name is *Anompoli Lawa.*"

St. John shook hands with the shaman. "David St. John, Doctor, my pleasure."

Stella smiled and also took his hand as did Peach.

"Heard a lot about you girls...and you, Captain St. John," said Winchester.

"How do you like our world, so far, Doctor?" asked Stella.

He smiled. "I'd rather not say, Stella."

She glanced around at the few people sunning themselves and the litter surrounding them.

"I think I understand."

"Ya'll hungry?"

"Funny you should ask, Peach," said Padrino.

"We brought some cheese burgers with bacon, curly fries and soda pops," replied Stella.

"Why don't we go up to Marshal McGann and my niece's log home just back up the trail so we can sit down, eat and visit," suggested Winchester.

Stella, Peach and the captain looked at each other.

"Uh...there's no log home back there, Doctor," said St. John. "There's two stone castles."

"Stone castles?" *Anompoli Lawa* frowned.

"Uh-huh, sweetie, a man named Collins built them in 1930 for his home. They're abandoned now, sorry," commented Peach. "But, there are some picnic areas just past there."

Padrino glanced over at the Shaman. "Forgot about that, Winchester or I would have mentioned it."

"Actually I should have expected that the house would no longer be there, after all I suppose it has been a hundred and twenty years," said the doctor as he nodded at Peach. "After you, my dear."

They turned and headed back around the trail the hundred yards to the castles, and then the picnic areas.

Stella picked a cedar picnic table with benches built on each side. "This should be okay."

They sat down on both sides and Peach took the burgers and drinks out of her bag and set them on the table.

A few people were walking by, headed toward the falls. A group of four, with one man, around twenty, in a faded blue, long sleeve T that had *Sometimes I'm So Cool I Can't Stand My Ownself,* printed in white on the front. His brown hair was moused and pushed into a center spike. He glanced over at St. John's group.

"Hey, look at the the old guy in the buckskins," he said to his friends, then he yelled over, "Old man, you goin' to a mountain man reenactor event?"

Winchester glanced down at his apparel and leaned over to Padrino. "I suppose I should have changed clothes before we came."

"Wouldn't have mattered," said St. John. "He's a bully type...just tryin' to look like a big shot to his friends."

"No different than in your time, Doctor," commented Padrino. "Just ignore him."

The bully walked over and set his cooler on the ground. "I'm talkin' to you, old man...You an Indian chief or somethin?"

"I suggest you go on with your friends, young man, and enjoy your day," intoned Padrino.

"Well, looky here, another old fart offering advice an' him playin' military in his cammo pants."

"Why don't you go on and leave us alone?" said Stella.

The man looked her up and down. "Hey, blondie, what's the deal, everybody at this table got a smart mouth?"

Padrino got to his feet and stepped over the bench to face the bully, and so did St. John.

The captain took the taller man by the arm and gently turned him away from the table and whispered to him, "I would suggest you move on, youngster...while you still can. That old guy in the buckskins isn't from around here and that knife in his belt is not there for decoration...The old fart, as you called him, doesn't have to play military...He's a retired, decorated, combat Marine...and trust me, kid, he's too old to take an ass whippin'...He'll just kill you before you can blink twice...Comprendo?"

The bully glanced at the dark eyes of *Anompoli Lawa*, and then at the gold-flecked amber ones of Padrino that were burning a hole in him.

He broke out into a sweat as the cold menace was evident in both. Then he glanced at his friends for backup—there was none coming.

Winchester slowly got to his feet to stand beside Padrino. The two men had wry grins on their faces.

The bully's eyes flicked back and forth like a rat trapped in a corner by a bobcat. "Uh...Sure, uh, hey, I was just jokin', didn't mean to bother ya'll."

He picked up his cooler, turned, and rejoined his friends over at the trail.

"Ya'll have a nice day...hear?" said St. John as they continued their way down to the falls.

Peach turned to Stella and grinned. "He doesn't know how close he came to havin' a knot jerked in his tail." She shook her head. "You just cain't polish a turd."

"I see human nature hasn't improved much," said Doctor Ashalatubbi as he sat back down.

"Not so you would notice," replied Padrino.

"Well, let's eat up,' commented Captain St. John as he unwrapped his burger.

The others followed suit.

Winchester got his unwrapped and looked at it for a moment. "Interesting...A fried meat sandwich." He looked at Stella. "You called these...cheeseburgers?"

She nodded. "Short for hamburgers with cheese."

"Ah, of course. In our time, we have German immigrants who fry ground meat patties...A standard meal for them."

Padrino took a bite of his, chewed it and swallowed. "Mmm...These are really good...The story goes, that a man named Fletcher Davis, of Athens, in east Texas, made fried meat sandwiches at his restaurant." He paused and took another bite. "Everyone called him Uncle Fletch...Well, seems he took his sandwich to the 1904 World's Fair in St. Louis and some local citizens, of Teutonic lineage, recognized the fried meat as a popular meal in their hometown of Hamburg..."

"And started calling it a 'hamburger'," finished St. John. He looked over at Winchester. "It's now the most popular food in the United States."

The Shaman took a bite of his burger. "Umm…They are tasty, I can understand why." He had a sip of his drink and nodded. "Phosphate or soda…also good."

"Been around since your time, honey, there's a whole bunch of 'em, but, we call 'em all 'cokes'."

Stella reached down by her foot, picked up Bone's go-bag and set it close to Padrino. "Here you go. All in there, plus plenty of ammo."

He unzipped it and glanced inside at the big Smith & Wesson 500.

"No such thing as plenty of ammo, Stella," said Padrino, smiling.

She nodded and added, "Right…Picked up a new Otis Elite Gun Cleaning kit from Buck Stienke down at Lone Star Shooting Supply."

"Howdy folks…Ya'll havin' a good time?"

They looked up at a large, barrel-chested man in a uniform—tan long sleeve shirt, dark olive drab pants, and a Smoky Bear hat. He had a Glock 19 on his belt. A silver badge on his shirt read, *Park Ranger*. His name plate said, *William Penny…*

§§§

CHAPTER TWELVE

TURNER FALLS - 1899

Bone peeked in the cave from the narrow pathway that ran behind the falls. He shined his powerful tac light all around, turned, and shook his head at the others standing on the bank next to some large rocks.

He managed to turn his bulk around and worked his way back to the bank.

"Gone, huh?" said Loraine.

"Even the deerskins they took in there to sit on," replied Bone.

"Just as well go on back up to the house…Don't 'magine there's anyway to tell how long they'll be," commented Jack. "Angiedarlin' probably has some lunch ready."

"Just hope they made it to our time and not somewhere else," added Bone.

"Guess we'll find out…eventually," said Loraine.

"Why don't ya'll try those telephoney things? suggested Bodie.

"Damn, now why didn't I think of that?" replied Bone as he took out his phone and the blue enigma crystal.

"Because Bodie thought of it first," said Loraine.

"Point, Pard." He held the crystal against the back of his Galaxy S7 and hit Padrino's speed dial number. There were several rings and then the circuit opened.

"Padrino," came the answer over the speaker.

"Take it ya'll made it," said Bone.

"Well, yes we did and we're here with Stella, Peach and Captain St. John...Also with a Park Ranger who has taken umbrage with your 500."

"Ooh, didn't think about that...Park Ranger, you say?"

TURNER FALLS - 2019

Padrino glanced up at the big man with silvered sunglasses towering over them at the picnic table. "Uh, yeah...a William Penny."

"William Penny? Will Penny?"

They looked up at him again.

"The Ranger nodded and shrugged. "My mother was a big fan of Charlton Heston, an' 'specially that western he did, *Will Penny*...So, since our last name was Penny...that's what she named me."

"Am I on speaker?" asked Bone.

"Uh, yeah," replied Padrino.

"Hey, Will, you old horse's ass, how you been?"

Penny pulled off his sunglasses. "Bone?...That you?"

"Does a bear crap in the woods?"

St. John and the others all exchanged puzzled looks.

"I'll be danged...Hadn't heard from you since the twenty year class reunion. How's your mama an' them?"

"They're good, Pard...You know that was my godfather, Padrino, that handed you the phone, don't you?"

Penny looked down. "Naw...Get out of town."

"Kid you not...Hey' ya'll, Will is my second cousin on my daddy's side...We went to high school together," came Bone's voice from the speaker.

Penny got a big grin on his face as he glanced down at Padrino and slapped him on the back. "Well, dog my cat, hadn't seen you since I was a little tike...You were still in the Corps."

"Oh, I remember you...You've grown a mite," said Padrino with a chuckle.

He grinned. "Yeah, seems like it."

"Say, 'bout that 500...That's my go-bag. I'm, uh...on a case an' they're...uh, bringing it to me."

"Really, what kinda case?"

"Aw, cuz, you know how it is...one of those...uh, undercover jobs. If I told you, I'd have to have Padrino kill you." Bone chuckled.

The big park ranger laughed, too. "Understand. Didn't see a thing...Hey, when you get it wrapped up, come up, we'll grab a beer."

"I'll hold you to that, cuz," said Bone. "Laterbye."

Will slipped his glasses back on and touched the brim of his campaign hat with his fingers. "Well, ya'll have a good day...an' keep that bag zipped up till you're out of the park. That damn hand cannon will scare some folks to death...Don't want to get my butt in a crack."

"No problem, Will, good to see you," replied Padrino.

The big man nodded once more. "Need to go check that bunch ya'll were talkin' to...bet they got beer in that cooler an' that's a no-no in my park." He headed toward the falls.

"Thanks, Bone, thought we were in trouble for a minute," said Padrino after Penny was gone.

"Aw, Will's an ok guy, little up tight sometimes...Good thing he's my cousin, the captain's badge wouldn't have meant much to him, bein' out of jurisdiction and all."

"Good point, Bone," said St. John. "When ya'll comin' back?"

"Hadn't decided yet. Sure is nice here. Lot less complicated...Not so many rules and regulations to deal with...an' these folks in this time period don't have a clue what political correctness is...Thank God."

"That's a good point, Bone. What do you want with your back-up 500?"

"Gonna give it to a Pinkerton detective we've been working with...Pretty little gal named Silke Justice."

"Silke Justice?" repeated Stella. "Wow, heard of her...Tough and salty...Not to be messed with. Been compared to Marshal Fiona Miller, uh...now, Fiona Flynn."

"The Chickasaw Nation just inducted her into their warrior clan. She's a Hatchet woman."

"Bless your heart, Silke, just read up some on the Hatchet women warriors...That possum's on the stump," said Peach.

TURNER FALLS - 1899

Silke got a puzzled look on her face and glanced over at Loraine, shook her head, and then shrugged her shoulders.

Bodie grinned and whispered, "Means it's as good as it gets...Heard my sweet Annabel say that a couple of times."

"Thank you, Peach, it is a great honor. They gave me a Chickasaw warhawk."

"Oh, guess now you'll have to learn how to use it," said Stella over the speaker.

"Already know how. Chickasaw Lighthorse Red Wolf has been teaching me some things over the last two years, includin' how to handle the tomahawk and Bowie knife...Now I'll have my own to practice with."

"Well, it's a lot quieter than a handgun, I'd say," commented St. John.

"Is that," replied Silke.

"When ya'll comin' back?"

"Be a little, bit, Bone, we're going to finish these cheese burgers and curly fries Peach and them brought us and visit a spell," said Padrino.

"Now that's one thing I do miss…cheese burgers and curly fries," added Bone.

"Want us to bring you one?"

"You know me too well, Padrino…Double meat, double cheese and bacon…all the fixin's with mustard…Oh, and curly fries, with ketchup."

Peach giggled. "See…ya'll?"

"What if Angie's got lunch fixed, Bone?" offered Loraine.

He grinned big. "You know me, Babe, been known to eat twice…Never know when you might miss a meal."

She shook her head. "Oh, God help me."

"How's married life treatin' ya'll?" asked Stella.

"We haven't killed each other…So far," replied Bone.

"Day's not over yet, Bone…Don't get cocky," commented Loraine.

"Well, now ya'll can kiss and make up."

"Ooh, good thought, Peach…Best part of havin' a fight."

Loraine popped the back of his head.

"What was that?" asked Stella.

"She just 'Gibbs' slapped me," replied Bone.

The sounds of both Stella and Peach giggling came through the speaker.

"Well, we'll see ya'll when you get back," said Jack. "Just come on up to the house."

"Laterbye," commented Bone as he hit the disconnect button.

TURNER FALLS - 2019

"Wait, wait...Damn you, Bone!" said St. John as he looked at the blank screen on the phone in Padrino's hand.

"What is it?" asked Stella.

"Need to find out if and when they're coming back," said St. John.

"Don't think they know, David. Like he mentioned, things are a lot less complicated back then. Law officers can actually do their jobs without having to constantly look over their shoulders at somebody or some legal-eagle organization wanting to sue them for some inane perceived violation of political correctness...or someone was offended by something," commented Padrino.

St. John nodded. "Like Belle Starr turning herself in just because she heard Bass Reeves had a warrant on her."

Padrino grinned. "Something like that...among other things."

TURNER FALLS - 1899

"See what you were talkin' about, Loraine,"

"About what?" she answered Silke.

"These doeskins...They're so comfortable. Like a second skin."

"Fiona said her grandmother's group only works with brain-tanned doe hides," added Loraine as they rounded the trail near the house.

"Isn't that Selden's horse, Dan, in the paddock next to the barn?" asked Bone as he noticed a big black Standardbred stallion munching on some hay.

"Who?" asked Silke.

"Deputy US Marshal Selden Lindsey, out of Ardmore," answered Loraine.

"Yeah, hadn't seen Selden since we nailed that gang that was goin' to kidnap and kill Teddy Roosevelt in the Kiamichis," said Bodie.

"Yep, sure enough, there the big son of a gun is sittin' on the porch drinking coffee," added Jack. "Must have known Angiedarlin' was fixin' a big lunch."

They opened the gate and headed to the porch.

"See ya'll finished the ceremony…Where's Winchester?" asked the broad-shouldered, black mustachioed, Lindsey as he got to his feet from a rocking chair.

"Long story," said Jack. "Selden, this is Pinkerton Detective Silke Justice and Texas Ranger Riley Boston…Think you know everbody else."

"Do."

Everyone howdied and shook Selden's hand.

"You lost, or just wantin' some of my Angiedarlin's cookin'?" asked Jack.

"Well, that too, but got a telegram for Miss Justice here." He reached inside his black morning coat, pulled out the yellow envelope, and handed it to Silke.

She opened it, removed the flimsy and read it. A intense frown came across her face as she took a deep breath. "Oh, Lordy, Lordy."

§§§

CHAPTER THIRTEEN

CHOCTAW NATION

"We'll cross Clear Boggy Creek an' head on up to the Shawnee Hills," said Duce. "Got a hideout in Choate Holler where we kin stay fer a spell." He chirked his horse up into an extended trot.

"Need to stop an' git some supplies," commented Mazeppa as he matched Duce's pace.

"We'll stop at Barnett, next to Grubb Mountain…Just this side of Coal Creek."

"Yer athinkin' they'll be sendin' out a posse, ain'tcha?" asked Goose.

"With what we done yesterd'y? What in hell do you think?"

"Mind yer right…When that train don't show at the next stop, they'll be asendin' somebody along the track to find out why," said Mazeppa.

"When we git to Muddy Boggy, we'll ride in the creek aways up to Caney Boggy to throw any trackers off…Got a good hard bottom most of the way," added Duce.

Goose laughed and shook his head. "Had no idee they was that much gold in double eagles in that safe…'long with the KATY payroll."

"Musta been sendin' the coin up the track to Kansas City from the depository in Dallas," said Mazeppa.

"How much you reckon they wuz all told?" asked Amos Logan from just behind his brother.

"If I wuz a bettin' man…I'd say better'n thirty thousand," replied Duce with a wry smile.

"Whoolaw! We'll paint the town and the front porch," said Amos.

"We'll do no such a damn thing...We'll let the fire cool off a spell first," snapped Duce.

TURNER FALLS - 2019

"How did ya'll get here?" asked Stella.

Padrino pulled out the *moldavite* crystal. "Same way I did when Captain St. John took me to the cave down at Possum Kingdom." He handed the crystal to Stella to look at. "When *Anompoli Lawa* told me about the spiral petroglyph in the cave behind the falls here...well, we thought we'd give it a try." He glanced at the doctor.

St. John shook his head. "That still amazes me and I wouldn't believe a bit of it if I hadn't seen it with my own eyes...twice now."

"Our people have legends of tribal members disappearing and of strange people appearing seemingly from nowhere...The stories go back to our ancients," said Winchester.

"When we first got ya'll on the phone, I didn't know whether to check my butt or scratch my watch," said Peach.

"What?" asked Stella.

"It's a southern thing, butter cup," Peach replied.

"Well, it was accidental...We just happened to be on the same ley line when we were in close proximity to the crystal in that statue and the *moldavite* in my pocket," commented Padrino.

"How did you know to use those communication devices?" asked Winchester.

"The what?...Oh, phones," said Stella.

"That was the funny thing," answered Padrino. "When we were next to the cave where that gold statue with the ruby crystal in it, we could smell exhaust from a gasoline engine, and then we could hear Tyrin barking."

"Oh, honey, he jumped out an' pitched a hissy fit over in front of that little bitty cave soon as we stopped the Gator."

"Beg pardon...Gator?" questioned Doctor Ashalatubbi.

"It's a motorized kind of a small buggy...Can go just about anywhere," replied Padrino. "We call it an all-terrain vehicle."

"Oh."

"Well, anyway, Tyrin was pitchin' this fit an' we could hear voices...almost like they were a long way off, but could still hear 'em...You know?" said Peach.

"We figured we were near one of those electromagnetic vortex things, so we got out our phones." Stella held up her Iphone. "I called Bone's number an' Peach called Padrino's...We both got through."

"Then they told us what to do with that gold statue, Honey Bunch." Peach glanced at Doctor Ashalatubbi. "I started doin' some research on those ley lines an' found there was one that ran from the great lakes to the Gulf of Cortez...an' just happened to go through the Arbuckles, Gainesville, an' Possum Kingdom." Peach giggled. "Well, I'm here to tell you, honey, made me happy as a dead pig in the sunshine, on account I knew long as we were along this line we could get in touch...or whatever."

"Plus, apparently the petroglyphs indicate electromagnetic hot spots." Padrino grinned. "I'd say that lends a lot of credence to Einstein's Special Theory of Relativity about the past, present, and future existing side-by-side in quantum entanglement...Spooky action at a distance."

"Excuse me?" questioned the doctor.

"Albert Einstein…"

He interrupted Padrino. "Ah, yes, the young German mathematician that everyone's been talking about."

Padrino nodded. "In 1921 he will be awarded the Nobel Prize for physics with his special and general theories of relativity…The special theory basically saying that time travel was possible…among other things."

"As I mentioned, our people have known this for millennia," said the doctor.

"Speaking of which, we might should see about heading back," commented Padrino.

"How do you know that you'll go back to the same place…and time?" asked Stella.

Padrino looked at her amber gold eyes, raised his eyebrows and smiled. "We don't."

MCGANN HOME

"What is it?" asked Loraine.

Silke sat down heavily at the top of the stoop, dismay and consternation were written on her face as she glanced down at the telegram again. Bear

Dog crawled over and put his chin on her leg and looked up at her face.

Silke glanced at Loraine, and then the others on the porch and pursed her lips. "Duce Walton has a gang now. They hit a KATY train at the jerkwater stop at Caddo."

"Get the payroll again?" asked Bone.

She paused for a moment and nodded. "Not only the payroll, but a shipment of double eagles in route to Kansas City...Thirty-five thousand dollars worth."

"Oh, my," said Loraine.

The others either whistled or groaned.

"Anybody hurt?"

Silke's gaze turned to Ranger Boston. "They shot the unarmed engineer and fireman down like dogs, and then killed the three men in the express car, the agent and two guards..."

"They try to fight?" asked Bone.

Silke shook her head. "They put dynamite under the car...and blew it up." She paused again and took a breath. "After...they took the money and gold out."

"After?" exclaimed Bodie.

"Why on earth would they do that for?"

"Apparently, Jack, they wanted plenty of time for their getaway...When the train didn't arrive in Atoka on schedule, the railroad sent a crew to see if she'd broke down," replied Silke.

"Send a posse out or anythin'?" asked Riley.

Selden nodded. "After the crew got back to Atoka...'Course the brigands had a six hour head start...They lost the tracks in Muddy Boggy Creek. Couldn't tell if they went upstream or down...Didn't have no Lighthorse to help 'em." He looked over at Red Wolf.

"I'm to go after them immediately." Silke glanced over at Riley. "Ranger Boston an' me, 'long with Red Wolf, that is...Know you don't have any jurisdiction in the Nations..."

"I can deputize him, far as that goes, Silke," said Selden. He glanced at Jack, Bone, and Loraine. "We can go along with you..."

Silke shook her head. "Move faster just the three of us. You know the logistics on a large posse is murder."

"She's got a point...Me an' Bass always tried to keep it down to just us when we were on a hot trail an' not just out servin' paper," commented Jack.

"We can always send a telegram for some help, once we got 'em penned down…"

Selden interrupted Silke. "Purty good idee, Detective." He looked at Red Wolf. "*Nashoba Hommá* moves right fast when he's on the track…He's in the same class as Bass."

Red Wolf nodded to Selden. "Uhh, work with big Lindsey, him know…lone dog run faster."

"They've moved the destroyed express car to the yard at Denison," added Selden.

Silke glanced at Red Wolf and Riley. "I want to take a look at that car before we go huntin' their trail…Do you know when the next train south to Gainesville is, Marshal Lindsey?"

"One this afternoon…" He pulled out his silver pocket watch from a vest pocket. "…in two hours. Don't think you can make that. Be 'nother in the mornin' at ten."

"That's doable. Maybe Padrino an' Doctor Ashalatubbi will be back later this afternoon."

"They'll be back in time for supper…Trust me," said Bone with a grin.

§§§

CHAPTER FOURTEEN

TURNER FALLS - 2019

St. John looked at his wristwatch. "Little after five o'clock…Park closes at six, doesn't it?"

"In the winter…right," answered Stella.

"We'd best go see if my crystal works as well going back as it did coming," said Padrino.

"I suspect you're right, my friend," replied Doctor Winchester as he got to his feet.

"I'll go get Bone's double-double an' curly fries an' meet ya'll down at the falls," added Peach as she also stood up.

St. John, Padrino, and Stella followed suit with Stella carrying the go-bag.

The four headed toward the falls while Peach walked over to the Onion Burger.

The sun was sitting just above the mountain top over the falls. Long shadows streaked across the large clear pool as the other park attendees gathered up their blankets, coolers, and lawn chairs. Most of their food wrappers and soft drink cans were left for the park stewards to pick up.

Anompoli Lawa led the way over to the large boulders on the north side of the falls, which shielded the group from prying eyes.

Stella handed the leather bag to Padrino as Peach walked up behind them with the white paper sack from Onion Burger. Doctor Ashalatubbi took it from her after she gave him a good hug.

Stella did the same to Padrino, and then stepped over to the Shaman as Peach embraced Padrino. St. John shook the hands of the two time travelers.

"Safe trip, gentlemen…If I didn't have to get home to my wife Sonjua, and our son, Damarcus, plus being up to my ass in alligators at the station, might just be tempted to go with ya'll." He turned to Stella and Peach. "And ya'll can't go either. I'm already shorthanded as it is."

"We know, we have to house and dog sit for Bone and Padrino, anyway. Wish we could have brought Tyrin with us, but they don't allow dogs in the park," said Stella.

Peach nodded. "Tyrin would have a duck fit if we left him with the Captain."

St. John looked at her. "Okay, what's a duck fit?"

She grinned. "That's one step above a hissy."

St. John rolled his eyes and shook his head.

"You can see if another call can go through when you get back to the ranch and close to the statue," Padrino said to the girls. "As Bone would say, 'Laterbye'."

He and *Anompoli Lawa* stepped over to the ledge that led behind the falls.

"Folks, almost closin' time," came a deep voice from behind St. John, Stella, and Peach…

MCGANN HOME - 1899

"Supper's on," said Angie from the screen door.

She had pulled her long flaming red hair back into a low-tied pony tail that draped over her right shoulder.

"Hot dang," replied Bodie. "Could eat the rear end out of a leather duck."

"And it's I'll be seein' if I can find ye one, Ranger. It's fried chicken, smashed potatoes, biscuits, sawmill gravy an' fresh saxifrage lettuce with yellow hop clover salad, the rest of us will be havin'," replied Angie as she opened the door to let everyone inside.

"Uh…that sure sounds better, Angie," Bodie replied with a big grin.

They all took their seats at the table after washing up and said their 'Amens' after Jack gave grace.

Angie glanced at Bone. "Do ye be thinkin' me uncle an' Padrino will be makin' it?"

Bone shrugged. "I would suppose. There's a lot about this time travel stuff we don't really understand, Angie…Heck, I don't really understand how we got here in the first place, not to say anything about Padrino showin' up."

"Don't forget about that criminal, Lenny Taylor, Honey," added Loraine.

"Him too…Must be some sort of regular pathway or channel between this time and back home, but danged if I can understand it…I guess it's like *Anompoli Lawa* said, 'If you journey to the past, then you are part of the past…'"

"And always have been," came a voice from the front screen door as it opened.

Everyone at the table turned as *Anompoli Lawa*, Padrino, and the three wolf-dogs came in.

"Faith an' praise be to sweet Jesus, ye made it back," said Angie as she got up from the table and hugged Winchester when they walked over to the table. "It was worryin' ye had me, Uncle."

He grinned. "The boys were sitting at the end of the ledge and met us as we came out from behind the falls…and the trip went off without a hitch…Well almost." He rubbed Son's head.

"'Almost' only works with horseshoes and hand grenades, Doc," said Bone.

"You can add time travel to that, then," replied Padrino. "Your cousin, Will Penny, the Park Ranger, showed back up just as we were stepping along the narrow ledge that led to the cave."

"Then how…" asked Loraine.

"He apparently didn't see us disappear behind the falls. We turned and looked back at him talking to St. John and the girls. Figured they would give him some kind of flimflam about where we were…so Padrino and I went on in and set down on our deerskins."

"We put Bone's burger and fries…and his go-bag between us, joined hands over the crystal and went into our meditative state," added Padrino. "Good thing we're both quite adept at it…and when we opened our eyes…We were back."

"Actually, we didn't know for sure until we peeked around the falls and didn't see anyone or any of the trash that had been laying around in that time," finished Doctor Winchester.

The three wolf-dogs were whacking the legs of Padrino and Winchester with their tails as they danced around the two men, happy to see them back.

"So how was your trip?" asked Bodie.

"*Veni, vidi, vici…*" said *Anompoli Lawa*.

"Uh-huh…Which means?" asked Bone.

"I came…I saw…I conquered," answered Silke. "It's a Latin phrase popularly attributed to Julius Caesar…My mother was a school teacher…Taught Latin and French…among other things."

Bodie shook his head. "You're just like Fiona. She's all the time quotin' somethin' from Shakespeare or Latin or that feller Confucius."

"If the shoe fits, then throw it at the wall," said Bone.

Bodie and Riley both looked at the big man and simultaneously said, "Huh?"

"It's a Bone thing," added Loraine.

"Well, it's sittin' yeselves down at me table an' it's some plates and silverware I'll be gettin' ye," said Angie as she turned and headed into the kitchen where the girls were having supper at their little table.

Winchester handed Bone the sack. He opened the top, stuck his face in and inhaled deeply. "Oh, golly, golly, golly, that smells good."

"You'll have to go by Marshal Loss Hart's new cafe he an Penny Weisman have opened in Ardmore…They call it the Burger Barn. Penny used to work for that feller, Uncle Dave, that invented those things down in Athens, Texas," commented Selden.

"Loss has a burger place in Ardmore? Wow, who knew?" asked Bone as he took a bite.

"Then it's guessin' I am that ye'll not be wantin' some of me chicken."

Bone held up both hands. "No, no, I'm a growin' boy, Angie."

"Surely ye'll not be havin' room for me apple cobbler then."

He flashed his big grin. "I think I can make room."

"Bone, there's no elastic in your buckskins, you know," said Loraine.

"Figure I'll work it off."

She reached over behind him and 'Gibbs' slapped the back of his head.

"Ow." He leaned over, lifted her chin with his index finger and gave her a sweet kiss on the lips.

"Damn you, Bone, you know exactly how to handle me, don't you?"

"I'm learnin', Darlin', I'm learnin'…Beats being thrown over your head again."

"What's this?" asked Silke.

"Kung Fu," replied Loraine.

"Ah, you haven't shown me that one, yet."

"First chance we get," said Loraine. "I'll demonstrate on Bone...It can come in right handy at times."

He held up his hands. "Uh-uh...Kings X, Baby. I give."

Padrino held up Bone's go-bag. "Got the 500, ammo, and a new cleaning kit the girls got from Buck Stienke down at his gun shop...There's also a Galco Dual Action Outdoorsman Holster and a cartridge belt that Stella said fit her...Ya'll are about the same size around the hips."

Bone didn't look up as he reached for a curly fry and dipped it in the puddle of ketchup from the usual small packet. "Yeah, she's got an onion butt, too."

"What's an onion butt?" asked Riley.

Bone took another bite of his double-double bacon cheese burger and answered as he chewed, "Make a man's eyes water."

Loraine popped him again.

Everyone laughed, including Silke, while Riley blushed.

"Looks like I'll be needin' it real soon," said Silke.

"Oh, developments?" asked Padrino.

Thirty minutes later, Padrino and Doctor Ashalatubbi had been filled in on the latest news brought up by Marshal Lindsey.

Angie moved around the long table, filling everyone's cup with her stout trail brew coffee.

Bone glanced at Silke as she looked over his spare, big 500. "When it gets light enough in the morning before we have to leave for town, we'll go outside and fire a few rounds. Let you get a good feel of the .50 cal."

"Good idea…The only time I fired yours was when I put one through Big John Tackett's brisket bone…an' that did the job," answered Silke.

"A .50 cal just about anywhere will usually drop a bad guy."

"I'm in the habit of puttin' my shots where I aim."

Anompoli Lawa grinned after he took a sip of the coffee from his white porcelain cup. "Red Wolf told me that *Kowishto' Ihoo Hommá*...Red Hair Woman, doesn't miss."

"That's an awfully big gun, Silke...Be hard to draw fast, I'm thinkin'...an' ye be no bigger than I," said Angie.

"You remember, Angiedarlin', that's about the same thing I told you before you shot those sticks of dynamite with your grandfather's ten gauge on the fly."

"Aye, it's rememberin' I am, husband...The blackguards were goin' to blow me house up."

Riley spoke, "It's not how fast you draw that counts...it's hittin' your target...First one that fires, usually misses, because they're hurryin' too much."

"Fiona told me that it's not the speed, but how you pull it an' fire in one smooth motion," said Bodie.

"I think you're both wrong," commented Loraine.

Bone leaned back in his chair and his enigmatic smile spread across his face.

"How so?" asked Riley.

"It's having the courage to draw and fire in the first place when you're facing deadly force." Loraine looked across the table at Silke. "You

Ken Farmer

should have seen her walking straight at Big John Tackett, with him pointing his .45 Colt at her chest and the hammer cocked...She never even slowed down, she just calmly raised Bone's big hand cannon in mid-stride...and blew the evil bastard away...Cool as a cucumber."

Silke pursed her lips. "You just do what has to be done."

§§§

167

CHAPTER FIFTEEN

TURNER FALLS PARK - 2019

Ranger Penny glanced around. "Where did Padrino and the other older fella in the buckskins go?"

"Oh, they left already," said St. John.

Will frowned. "That can't be, I've been between here and the entrance all afternoon…Since I first talked to ya'll."

Peach grinned and blinked her long black eyelashes at the same tempo as her voice, "My, my, my, honey, you could be lost as last year's Easter eggs tryin' to keep up with those two…You already know that Padrino is a retired combat Marine an' his friend…*Anompoli Lawa*? Just happens to be a Chickasaw Shaman…An', darlin', if either one of 'em don't want to be seen…why, there just isn't a man alive gonna see 'em…Hear?" She giggled. "That dog just ain't gonna hunt." Peach reached up and tugged gently on his earlobe.

Penny blushed and stammered, "Uh…right…Uh, didn't know that 'bout the other fellow…uh, bein' a Shaman, I mean."

Peach hooked his elbow with hers. "Precious, why don't you walk with us to our car. Betcha you've never seen Bone's 1930, L-29 Cord Cabriolet."

His brown eyes got big. "Bone has a 1930 Cord? Oh, damn!"

He strode toward the path back up to the parking area, almost dragging Peach along. She glanced back at Stella and St. John just behind them and winked.

MCGANN HOME - 1899

The big golden orb peeked over the top of the tree covered ridge on the east side of Honey Creek valley.

The McGann's rooster had sounded his morning greeting a good hour earlier, even before the eastern sky began to turn pink. He was strutting around the yard between the house and barn, making sure all his harem was out of the coop and scratching the ground for worms, seeds, and insects.

Angie came out of the barn with a galvanized two gallon bucket with their morning chicken scratch. She walked over among the hens and pullets and started scattering handfuls of the cracked grain around.

"Here, chick, chick, chick…come chick, chick. Whoo…chick. Come an' get ye breakfast."

The brood gathered around her trying to be first to go after the crushed, corn, milo, and oat morsels as they hit the ground.

She emptied the bucket, headed back to the barn to put it up, and then walked to the house.

Bone had the Smith & Wesson 500 disassembled with the pieces laying on a washed flour sack towel on the kitchen table.

Everyone else was sitting around with their after breakfast coffee watching him instruct Silke on how to take the .50 caliber handgun apart, clean, and put it back together. He removed the blindfold from around her eyes.

"Good job, kid. It's always a good thing to be able to take your weapon apart and put it together without lookin'. You might have to do it in the dark at some time…or another."

Riley was giving the inside of her leather holster a good coating of butter to soften it and allow it to mold to the shape of the big gun.

Bone slipped the belt through the slots on the back and then filled the twenty loops sewn on the belt with the big 500 grain .50 cal cartridges.

"Now you can wear it on your right side or the left in front of your hip in a cross draw…Whatever you prefer."

"Think I'll do the cross draw so I can use my left hand to unsnap that hold-down strap and draw with my right…Should be a little quicker, that way."

"I can agree with that," replied Bone.

He showed her how to grip the weapon and a modified Weaver shooting stance.

"This gives you better balance and a stable platform for shooting," he said as he demonstrated a two-handed grip.

"Double-action isn't it?" she asked Bone.

"Uh-huh, but sometimes it compounds the fear of the person looking down the barrel of this big son of a buck to hear the double click when you cock the hammer manually...It's a deterrent on its own." His grin spread across his face.

"Let's go make some music," Silke suggested.

"Works for me," Bone replied as he picked up the rest of the box of ammo. "Angie, you got a can we can have?"

"Aye, Bone, ye can have this empty Royal Bakin' Powder container."

Angie handed him the square tin of baking powder she had emptied that morning making the pancakes. It was six inches high, by four wide, by three inches deep, and red with white lettering.

"Got string?" he asked.

"Ye can look in the top drawer of me hutch over by the door."

He walked over, opened the drawer and took out a small ball of cotton twine, unrolled about two feet and cut it with Angie's paring knife from the counter.

He and Silke headed to the front door, followed by everybody else.

Bone took his pocket knife, punched a hole in the side of the tin near the top. He took the string, ran the end through the hole and tied it off.

Bone stepped off about forty feet to a large winter bare red oak and tied the other end of the string around a branch that was about head high to the big man. He turned and walked back to the porch.

Everyone had taken seats in the chairs about the porch, including the five foot wide swing hung by chains from the ceiling, where Winchester and the girls sat.

Bone and Silke stood side-by-side just above the steps.

"All right, kid, that's about forty feet...Let's see if you can hit it."

He turned to everyone else on the porch. "Ya'll need to cover your ears or stick your fingers in them and open your mouths, this puppy is pretty loud…You young ladies use your fingers."

Bone held out his hand to Silke. "Here, these are ear plugs. There's a box of them in my go-bag…Come in handy when you're practicin'."

She took the two soft yellow plugs and inserted them in her ears like Bone had just done.

Bone shouted, "Firing."

Everyone held their hands over their ears while Aurali Red and Baby Sarah stuck their index fingers in theirs and opened their mouths.

"Don't draw, just use that two-handed grip and stance I showed you, sight, cock, and fire," he told her.

Silke dropped her right foot behind her left about twenty inches, pointed her toe out at a forty-five degree angle, put most of her weight on her front foot and leaned forward a little. She bent her knees slightly, raised the 500 straight out from her right shoulder, wrapped her left hand underneath the heel of her right in the two-handed grip and dropped her left elbow.

Silke thumbed the hammer back, pointed the gun at the can and squeezed the trigger. The explosion was terrific. A ball of fire momentarily appeared at the muzzle as the can under the tree spun around and swung back and forth.

"Again," said Bone.

She did as he instructed, a little smoother this time.

"Again," he commanded.

She fired the three shots in a little over three seconds.

"You got two rounds left. Fire them without cocking the hammer," said Bone.

Again, she did as he instructed—the second shot missed.

"See, you have to compensate for not only the recoil, but the additional leverage you have to use to pull the trigger to cock the hammer."

"Wow, yes, I do see...It really makes me feel more powerful, though, knowing whatever I hit is goin' down."

"Now reload using that speed loader I gave you and we'll try something else."

She took out her speed loader from her possibles bag that had come with her new doeskins, removed the spent rounds and inserted five more.

"Not bad...thirty seconds. You'll get better."

Bone drew his 500, fired at the can, grazing the side, causing it to swing side to side and spin around.

"Now, while it's moving…all five rounds."

"Oh, goodness."

She watched the can oscillate for a short beat and then squeezed the trigger.

The can spun crazily. The second shot sent it in the opposite direction and the third spun it back, the forth up in the air and the fifth sent it over the top of the branch and back down the front side.

Everyone on the porch oohed and aahed and applauded.

"All right kid, way to go," said Bone as he patted her shoulder.

"Now let's draw for time…Remove your empties…Put it in your holster and snap the strap."

Silke nodded and did as he ordered. She snapped and unsnapped the strap a few times and then signaled she was ready.

"Go."

She unsnapped the strap with her left just as her right grabbed the grip, pulled the weapon from the holster and cocked the hammer. Silke simultaneously dropped her right foot back, flexed her knees as she brought the .50 cal on target, stabilized it with her left hand and squeezed the trigger for a dry fire.

"Little under a second." He looked at the dive watch on his wrist. "Not bad for the first time. This is one of those things you have to practice until you have it ingrained as muscle memory...In other words...Automatic...You have to do it without thinking," said Bone. "Now...live."

Silke reloaded the 500 and nodded to Bone. She looked out at the can. It was almost hanging in tatters—pounded flat and full of big holes.

She grinned. "Not big as it was."

"Uh-huh," replied Bone, he matched her smile, and cut his eyes at Loraine.

"Go," Loraine shouted from the end of the porch.

Silke popped the strap loose, drew and fired all in one motion. The can snapped away from the string and bounced ten feet into the brush behind the tree.

"Seven tenths of a second...Little Bit. Not bad...With more practice, should get it down to three tenths or so...Now pick up your brass so you can get them reloaded."

Silke pulled the soft yellow plugs from her ears. "One other advantage I see is there's no smoke for somebody to shoot back at."

"No, but at night the muzzle flash will damn near light up the sky," said Bone.

"Here's hoping you'll never have to use it, child," said *Anompoli Lawa*.

She looked over at the venerable Chickasaw Shaman and nodded. "I'd rather have it and never use it than need it an' not have it."

"Franz Kafka, the German novelist said something very similar," said Padrino. "'Better to have, and not need, than to need, and not have'."

"Think she just said that," commented Bone.

§§§

CHAPTER SIXTEEN

SANTA FE DEPOT
GAINESVILLE, TEXAS

The southbound Gulf and Colorado locomotive braked to a stop at the platform, venting steam from both sides of the big boiler.

Faye Skeans met the group as they disembarked from the second passenger car.

Silke was off first, leading Bear Dog on a leash. Loraine followed her, with Bone and the others behind her.

She led the gangly half-grown pup over to a grassy area on the north end of the depot and let him water a bush. Then they went back where Faye was greeting the others.

"Buggy is out front." She noticed Silke's formfitting outfit. "Love your new doeskins, Silke...beautiful."

"So comfortable, too, Faye," replied Silke as she and the older woman hugged.

"Let me take one of those bags, honey. Looks like you've added one since you left." She took the carpet bag and let the younger woman carry the leather go-bag. "See you also got some new armament...That's just like Bone's...How?"

She grinned. "Tell you when we get to the boardin' house."

Faye hugged Padrino for what seemed to be a much longer time than the others—the retired Marine didn't seem to mind.

"Happy you're back, Jethro," said Faye.

"Happy to be back, sweet Faye."

"Oh, go on with you," she smiled as her fingertips brushed his cheek.

They loaded up in Faye's two seat surrey and headed to her boarding house.

SKEANS BOARDING HOUSE

"...and that's pretty much it, Faye. Doctor Ashalatubbi and I made it back to this time with no hitches." Padrino grinned as he sipped some of her stout coffee. "He wasn't impressed with how the world progressed or maybe he would say regressed in my time...It wasn't hard to disagree with him."

"I would have been a nervous wreck if I had known you and the good doctor were goin' to do that," said Faye.

"Once he told us there was a spiral petroglyph in the cave behind the falls signifying a portal...seemed like the thing to do since Silke wanted a gun like Bone's so badly."

"Riley an' I are headin' to Denison in the mornin', Faye. Meetin' Red Wolf at the train yard," said Silke, changing the subject.

"We need to get on the trail of those miscreants, ma'am. They kilt five men in this last robbery for no reason…'cept to slow any posse down," added Riley.

Faye brought her hand to her mouth. "Oh, goodness, how terrible." She looked at Padrino. "You're not going, are you, Jethro?"

"Not yet, sweet lady. They can track faster with fewer people. If they run the brigands to ground, they can send for Bone, Loraine and I." He glanced over at Silke for her nod.

She smiled and winked at him.

"Don't leave me out of this dance," quipped Bodie.

Riley looked over at the big rawboned ranger. "Wouldn't think of it, pard."

Faye smiled and looked back at Padrino. "Oh, good, I wanted to make you a parlor jacket while you're here. I've already bought some Japanese silk for it."

"Why, Faye, how nice. Don't think I've ever had anyone make anything like that for me."

"Then it's about time."

KATY DEPOT

Silke led *Lakna'*, her line-back dun gelding, down the cleated ramp from the stock car of the east bound Santa Fe train from Gainesville. Riley was right behind her with Duke, his blood bay, almost black, gelding.

Red Wolf waited for them at the bottom of the ramp with the railroad hostler.

"Unnn…Train on time," said Red Wolf.

"Let's water the boys an' then go over an' take a gander at that express car," commented Silke.

"I'll take 'em to water, ma'am. Won't be no trouble…no trouble atall," offered the young, cotton-headed, KATY employee."

"Much obliged," replied Silke as she flipped him a Morgan silver dollar.

He snatched the coin in the air. "Wow, thankee, ma'am," the hostler said as he grabbed the two horses reins and led them toward a water trough next to one of the pens.

Red Wolf nodded at her, turned and headed down the tracks to the yard where the wrecked car had been dragged. They trailed along behind him with Bear Dog padding at Silke's side.

The three noticed a young girl in a faded calico dress standing beside what was left of the express car as they walked up.

Silke and Riley exchanged glances as they watched her shoulders shake, and then she bent down and laid some handmade paper flowers on the bent frame of the express car.

Silke approached the nine year old girl and gently placed her arm around her shoulder. "What's wrong, honey?"

The blond-headed child turned her tear streaked face up to Silke. "I...I had to make flowers out of...of paper...There's just not..." her voice broke as she choked back a sob that racked her frail little body. "...not 'ny real ones this time of...of year," her voice broke as she sniffed and wiped her arm across her running nose.

Silke pulled a clean handkerchief from her possibles bag and handed it to her.

Bear Dog laid down beside the child, with his muzzle between his paws

The little girl wiped her eyes and then blew her nose, looked up again as the tears continued to roll from her big blue eyes and nodded her thanks.

"Were you related to one of the men who were in this car?"

Her face scrunched up with emotion as she choked back another sob. "Uh-huh…My…my daddy…my daddy…my daddy…." She broke down again. The tears were coming from her very soul.

She almost collapsed to her knees, but Silke caught her, knelt down and gathered the devastated child to her bosom.

The girl's tears came afresh, shaking her entire body with sobs as Silke held her tight. Bear Dog placed his muzzle across her little foot and looked up at her.

"I'm so sorry, honey…Let it go…Let it all go," Silke whispered to her as tears ran down her face as well.

She held her for over five minutes until the little girl couldn't cry any more. The handkerchief Silke had given her was soaked.

"What's your name, honey?" Silke asked.

She took a breath. "Elizabeth, but…but my daddy…my daddy called me…'Lizabeth."

"Was your daddy the express agent?"

Lizbeth nodded. "He had been with the railroad since 'fore I was born." She sniffed again. Bear Dog nuzzled her hand and licked it.

Riley stepped over and offered her a dry hanky.

She looked up at the handsome ranger, nodded and tried to smile.

"I...I wanted to bring him real flowers...but..." The tears began to flow again.

Silke eased the girl back at arms length and two sets of blue eyes looked at each other. "Lizbeth, I promise we'll find the men who did this...Hear me? I promise."

"Are you marshals?"

"No, honey, my name is Silke, Silke Justice. I'm a Pinkerton detective working for the railroad...this is Texas Ranger Riley Boston an' that's Lighthorse Red Wolf over there." She pointed at the Chickasaw law officer standing off to the side in respect.

Lizbeth turned back to Silke. "Why did they kill...kill my daddy?...Why?...Why? He never hurt nobody," her voice broke again.

"Because they are evil men, Lizbeth...They're just plain evil."

"Mama...Mama says she doesn't know what we're gonna do now." She caught her breath and sobbed again.

Silke and Riley exchanged glances, knowing what each was thinking.

She pulled Lizbeth close to her again and hugged her tight. "Honey, tell her not to worry. God will provide...I promise you. Tell her that, will you?"

She sniffed again and nodded.

"Where is your mama?" Silke asked.

"She's to home...Cain't get out of bed...I had to come see papa." Another sob escaped her chest. "We live just a couple blocks thataway." She nodded toward the east.

Silke reached in her possibles bag and took out five gold double eagles and started to hand them to her.

Riley touched her shoulder and gave her five more from his pocket.

Silke smiled, wiped the tears from her own eyes, and nodded. She turned back to Lizbeth and handed her the two hundred dollars in gold coins. "Here, baby, you take this to your mama and tell her there will be more coming...You do that, hear?"

Lizbeth looked at the ten double eagles, she had to hold with both hands, with a puzzled expression. "I don't understand."

Bear Dog nuzzled her again and she knelt down and hugged the black pup. He licked her face, bringing a little smile.

Silke also smiled and kissed the child on the forehead. "You put that money in your pocket and trust in the Lord, honey…He will provide."

§§§

CHAPTER SEVENTEEN

ATOKA, IT

Silke, Riley, and Red Wolf had unloaded at the KATY Depot and were trotting northwest along the Muddy Boggy to cut sign of the Walton gang.

The sheriff's posse out of Atoka had tracked the gang to the creek and lost the trail there.

"Horses enter creek here," said Red Wolf.

They were seven miles northwest of Atoka when Red Wolf held up his hand to stop at the bank of the Muddy Boggy.

"Which way did they go, back south, or north?" asked the ranger.

"Go north. See moss gone in places on rock bottom. Easy track," Red Wolf replied.

"How many you make it?" asked Silke

Red Wolf held up both hands, then closed both to fists and held up one finger.

Silke nodded. "Eleven…Let's split up an' take both sides until we find where they came out," she said. "Riley, you, me an' Bear Dog, will take the west side…Red Wolf, you got the east."

Red Wolf waded his red Appaloosa with a white blanket on his rump across the creek. It was only belly deep on the gelding.

Silke and Riley headed northwest at a slow trot, scanning the wooded bank for any sign the outlaws had left the creek. Bear Dog padded along, occasionally stopping to smell of some coon scat or a rabbit trail—he had the curiosity of any young canine.

At twelve miles northwest of Atoka, Red Wolf approached the confluence of Caney Boggy with the Muddy Boggy. He stopped and studied the area carefully, and then whistled like a Bob White.

"That's Red Wolf," said Silke. "Come on."

She nudged *Lakna'* through the trees that bordered the Muddy Boggy and down into the creek. Bear Dog followed alongside her, paddling and occasionally lapping up some water as he swam. Riley waded Duke in behind them across the seventy foot wide waterway.

They worked their way through the woods, where the trees were just showing signs of budding, on the northeast side, and then turned to the north around two hundred yards where Red Wolf was waiting.

"Cut sign, Red Wolf?" asked Silke as she reined up beside him.

"Unnn, gang still in water, but go up Caney Boggy."

A grin came across Silke's face. "Dollar to a bear sign, they're headed to Barnett for supplies."

"You're sayin' we shouldn't track 'em anymore?" asked Riley.

She shook her head. "Somethin' I learned from Bass Reeves…It's better to go where they're goin' than try to follow their trail. Barnett is the only place to get supplies between McAlester and the Canadian River…Other than a little wide spot in the trail called Legal…It's kinda similar to Slapout."

"What's Slapout?" Riley inquired.

"Another one horse town up in the Cherokee Strip."

"Why do they call it that?"

She grinned. "Well 'cause the storekeep there at the only store in town would all the time say, 'Sorry…slap out of that'."

He smiled back. "You're funnin' me."

Silke shook her head. "Would I kid you?…Let's go."

She bumped *Lakna'* into a medium trot just slow enough that Bear Dog could keep up.

Red Wolf almost got a grin on his face as he trotted behind her.

Riley sat where he was, taking a moment trying to decide if he was being had or not. He finally kicked Duke into a lope to catch up—still not knowing.

He eased his gelding back to a medium trot to match Silke's. "How far to Barnett?"

"Oh, 'bout a spit an' a promise."

"Huh?"

She shook her head and giggled. "A little less than twenty miles…Won't make it today. We'll camp alongside Caney Boggy near White Chimney."

"Nope, not gonna ask, just not gonna," said Riley shaking his head.

Silke looked over at him and smiled.

CHOATE HOLLER

"Mushy, you take first watch down at the south end of the holler, Dog'll relieve you in three er four hours," said Duce.

"Hows come I gotta be first?"

"'Cause I said so, that's why…'Sides yer closer to the horses."

Mushy glanced over his shoulder at the horses. "Oh, right," he grumbled.

"We only need one guard?" asked Mazeppa.

"Uh-huh, only two ways into this holler…from the north an' from the south. We got anybody on our tail, they be comin' from the south." Duce cut a chunk from his twist of Brown's Mule and stuffed it in the side of his mouth. "Ridges an' hogbacks er too rough on the east an' the hills on the west is bordered by the Canadian…Ain't no way to cross, 'sides a ferry, this time of year."

He worked the chew around and spat his first long stream of the viscous, amber fluid on a log in the fire. It popped and sizzled, and then bubbled away in a small cloud of steam.

"See yer point," said Mazeppa Logan.

His brother, Amos, fished a bottle of whiskey from his saddlebags, leaned back against a large rock and pulled the cork. He took a healthy swallow.

"Hey, how 'bout some of that forty rod?" said Paden, as he held his hand out. "Just as well get a little lubrication…we gonna be here awhile."

CANEY BOGGY CREEK

"This looks good," said Silke as she reined up at a glade next to the creek. "Got some winter grass, vetch, an' yellow hop clover graze for the horses an' some rocks big enough to hide our fire."

"Good idea, no need in advertisin' we're here," added Riley.

"Red Wolf go hunt for meat." He pulled his short war bow and quiver of arrows from its sleeve on his saddle. "No make noise."

He dismounted and stripped the tack from his Appy.

"We'll rub him down, Red Wolf, you go on," said Silke.

The Lighthorse nodded and disappeared into the heavier woods that ran alongside the creek.

"He's like a ghost, idn't he?" commented Riley.

"Yep, don't see him 'less he wants you to."

The sun was settling just above the westernmost ridge of the Shawnee Hills. Streaks of red ran between the few cirrus clouds on the horizon that had bright silver linings.

Silke glanced to the west. "Be a little nippy tonight."

"Think so?"

"Uh-huh...I'll dig a fire pit over against that boulder underneath that big Holly. Block any light to the north an' scatter any smoke...You mind pullin' the tack an' seein' to the boys?" she asked.

"No problem...Go to gatherin' some driftwood when I finish...Should be plenty of dry that won't smoke much, anyway."

Silke stripped some phloem from the inside of a slab of cedar bark from a long dead tree. She wadded the brown fibers in her hands and then rubbed them together until she had a coarse powder.

The punk made an excellent fire starter when placed under a small teepee of twigs.

Silke took a wax-coated Lucifer from the beaded parfleche hung across her chest, struck it on one of the rocks she had placed around the one foot deep pit and held it to the powder. The edges smoldered for a moment and then caught, sending a yellow flame up into the twigs.

She started adding larger sticks of deadfall to the growing flame, and then some broken limbs that Riley stacked beside the pit.

He brought in an armful of bigger driftwood he had broken up and laid it on the pile. "That should last the night."

Silke placed their blue merle graniteware coffee pot on one of the flat rocks surrounding the fire.

"Should be boiling in a few minutes," she said.

"Could use some," replied Riley.

They both looked up as Red Wolf entered camp from a small game trail that ran along the creek through the woods. He had a field-dressed young doe slung over his shoulder.

"Hey, venison steaks for supper...uh-huh," said Riley.

"Unnn, find barren doe, be tender...Red Wolf cut up."

He stepped over to a nearby white oak, took a long piggin' string from his possibles pouch and hung the carcass by the heels from a head-high limb.

"Water's boilin'," commented Silke as Red Wolf started skinning the doe while Bear Dog sat nearby watching and patiently waiting for his supper.

She dumped two handfuls of Arbuckles in the pot. "Be ready when it boils again."

An hour later, they sat around the fire with their after dinner coffee.

"The grilled steaks were awesome, madam," said Riley as he took a sip from his cup. "As is your trail brew."

Red Wolf had cut a bunch of the venison into long, thin strips and had it hung over the smoldering fire on a green willow rack he made.

"Jerky be ready by mornin', Red Wolf rub pepper on it," he said.

"Love peppered jerky," commented Silke.

Bear Dog was sound asleep at Silke's feet, his belly full.

The normal night sounds of frogs and an occasional owl was suddenly pierced with a shrill woman-like scream.

Silke and Riley jumped.

"*Kowishto'*," said Red Wolf.

"What?" asked Riley.

"Panther," replied Silke.

"Never heard one before," he said. "*Seen* plenty in south Texas, though."

"Red Wolf take rest of carcass down stream. *Kowishto'* smell. Him hungry…Not good let go waste…Meby *nita'* come."

"*Nita'*?" asked Riley with a perplexed look.

"Bear," answered Silke. "Bear Dog is *Nita' Ofi'*, in Chickasaw."

The half-grown pup raised his head and glanced at Silke when she mentioned his name, and then promptly laid his head between his paws, sighed, and went back to sleep.

Across the creek, a pack of coyotes began tuning up with their night song. Bear Dog raised his head again, looked across the creek, and a low growl emanated from his throat.

"Well, know one thing," said Silke.

"That would be?" asked Riley.

"With all the major predators out an' about tonight, there shouldn't be any two-legged creatures around anywhere nearby."

"Wouldn't count on that little lady," came a voice from the east side camp, nearest the trail—downwind.

§§§

CHAPTER EIGHTEEN

CANEY BOGGY CREEK

A silver-templed, tall man, wearing a tan canvas belted hunting jacket with brown leather elbow patches, entered the camp. He was carrying a Mauser Model 1895 bolt action rifle, held loosely in the crook of his right arm and wore a gray herringbone tweed Irish Walker hat.

"Smelled your smoke…and then your coffee," he said.

"Mister McPherson! What are you doin' out here?" asked Silke.

He smiled, flashing his even white teeth. "On a hunting trip…It's an annual thing. Need to get some alone time away from the saloon," he answered, referring to the Painted Lady Saloon and Restaurant in Gainesville.

"And call me Tim, please…You're that Pinkerton detective, Silke Justice, aren't you?…As I recall, ya'll came in the Painted Lady with Bone and Loraine last week."

"Guilty as charged…This is Texas Ranger…"

"Riley…?"

"Boston, uh…Tim," the ranger interrupted.

"Yes, of course."

"Would you care for some coffee?…We've eaten, but I can grill you up a venison steak, if you like," said Silke.

"Well, at the risk of imposing, I'll say yes to both…I was looking for a good place to camp when I smelled your fire," Tim replied with a hint of a Boston accent.

"Shuck that duffle on your back, you're welcome to camp with us," added Riley. He noticed McPherson had a Nagant M1895, seven round handgun strapped high around his hips in a flap-over holster.

"That's so very kind of you."

Tim slipped the pack from his shoulders. Opened the top and took out a green-speckled graniteware cup and handed it to Silke.

"What are you all doing out this way?...If you don't mind my asking."

He looked up as Red Wolf entered the camp from the shadows near the creek and jumped. "Oh," he exclaimed.

Silke glanced over at the Chickasaw and smiled. "This is Lighthorse *Nashoba Hommá*...Didn't see you leave, Red Wolf."

"Hear sound, not animal, Red Wolf go in shadows," he holstered his Colt .44-40 as he spoke.

McPherson smiled. "Gave me a bit of a start, my good man."

Red Wolf sat down where he had been earlier and picked up his cup from behind a rock where he had set it. "Unnn...Red Wolf always careful."

"I see...Good practice out here, I would say."

"To answer your question, Tim, we're on the trail of some lowlife, murderin' train robbers," said Silke as she filled his cup and handed it back to him.

"Oh?" He took a sip of the coffee after blowing across the top and licking the edge of the cup to cool it.

"Goodness, you brew an excellent cup of coffee, my dear."

"Thank you, kind sir." She tilted her head toward him.

"They killed five men on a northbound KATY south of Atoka," commented Riley.

"Left a beautiful nine year old girl without a daddy...Daughter of the express agent," added Silke as she flexed her jaw muscles and her blue eyes took on a flinty chatoyant glimmer in the flickering firelight.

"How terrible," responded Tim. "Well, I certainly hope you catch the villainous cretins."

"No hope to it," said Silke.

She laid a thick venison steak from the doe's backstrap in the skillet with some bacon drippings, sprinkled it with a pinch of salt, and then some ground pepper from a small cotton bag.

"Mmm, smells scrumptious," said McPherson as the steak began to sizzle on the cast iron. "Too bad we don't have some red wine to go with it." He winked at Silke.

"Bad planning on our part," she replied, blushing.

"That's a Nagant pistol, isn't it?" asked Riley.

Tim nodded. "Yes, it is…7.62 caliber. A gift from my father."

"Seven rounds?" said Riley.

"Yes…Very perceptive. You must be a weapons aficionado, Ranger."

"Goes with the territory."

"I must confess, I'm not very good with it. Just carry it for snakes and such."

"Never fired one…Heard they were a good weapon."

"Very sturdy. The cocking mechanism turns the cylinder, of course, but then moves it forward. That closes the gap between the cylinder and the barrel preventing the escape of the gases…not to say anything of increasing the velocity…Used by Russian army officers…I'm told."

"Interestin'," replied Riley.

McPherson glanced over and noticed the 500 on Silke's left hip. "My, my, that's a gun like Mister Bone carries, isn't it?"

"Yes, Bone gave me this one…It's a Smith and Wesson….50 cal."

She flipped the steak over where it sizzled afresh in the hot skillet.

"Big gun for a lady," he commented.

"I can handle it," she replied with a wry grin.

"I'm sure you can…I wasn't aware they were generally available," said Tim.

"They're…uh…experimental, or so Bone tells me…uh, knows someone at the company, I think."

Bear Dog raised his head and looked at Silke, and then at McPherson and cocked his head.

"How do they shoot?" he asked, and then took another sip of his coffee.

"Loud," interjected Riley.

"I hit what I aim at…It only takes one."

"I can imagine." He looked down at Bear Dog. "Is that a wolf?"

"Wolf dog…He adopted me," replied Silke. "He's already quite protective."

"Looks like he's going to be very large."

"That's what Bone said."

Silke stuck a fork in the steak, laid it in a tin plate and handed it to Tim. "That should be about right."

"I'm sure it is."

The half-grown pup continued to stare at McPherson with his blue eyes.

"He has intense eyes," he commented as he took the plate and fork from Silke, and then removed a Barlow folding knife from his jacket pocket.

"I'd say...He's very perceptive and seems to know what I'm thinkin'." She looked down at him and rubbed the top of his head.

CHOATE HOLLER

Most of the gang had finished their beans and bacon and the fried hot water cornbread that skinny as a rail, Herky, had fixed.

"What about the boss man?" asked Mazeppa.

He got to his feet, grabbed the tin coffee pot with one of his folded over gloves and filled his cup.

"What about him?" replied Duce as he took a sip from his own.

"Thought you had to go meet him." Mazeppa sat back down on a log.

"Changed my mind," replied Walton.

Mazeppa cocked his head and stared at Duce for a long moment. "You said a while back that he weren't a feller to mess with."

Walton stared back at the older of the Logan brothers. "Suggest you mind your own business, Mazeppa. I'll take care of the doin' 'round here."

A wolf howl echoed off the sides of the holler from the north end.

"Check on the horses, Dirt," said Duce.

"You got it," said the grubby little man.

CANEY BOGGY CREEK

"Where's your horse?" asked Riley.

"Back downstream a little bit. Was trying to be quiet. Need to go tend to him and get my bedroll." Timothy got to his feet.

"Go ahead an' finish your supper." Silke turned to the Chickasaw. "Red Wolf, would you go fetch Mister McPherson's horse an' put him with ours…What with that cat out prowlin', he doesn't need to be by himself."

"Oh, good idea, Silke, forgot about the puma. Heard him a bit ago…I was so entranced in visiting with you." He glanced at Red Wolf. "He's down…"

The Lighthorse was already walking toward the darkness. "Me find."

Timothy watched the Indian disappear into the night. "Doesn't talk much, does he?"

"No, but when he does, a person would be wise to listen," replied Silke. "He's been my mentor for the last two years…except for when I worked with Bone, Loraine, Padrino, and Bass Reeves."

McPherson paused in mid chew, and then finished and swallowed. "He's a real legend. Hear he's about the best there is in the Marshal's office."

"No about to it…Whatever you've heard is only half of it…Trust me on that…He even arrested his own son."

McPherson nodded. "Knew about that. The young man worked for me a while until his father tracked him and Tom Story down at a big race we had in Gainesville a few years ago."

"Oh, that's the one where Marshal Farmer got shot, isn't it?" asked Silke.

"The shot just glanced off his ribs, but he fell out of the observation tower at the track and broke his leg."

"I thought he got shot in the leg," commented Silke.

Mcpherson shook his head and took a bite of fry bread. "Basically a flesh wound, just landed wrong, but he's tough as boot leather...Now, if any ne'er-do-well messes with him..." He grinned. "...he'll just whack them with his bull penis cane."

Silke laughed and blushed again.

McPherson's steel gray eyes focused on her *Aphrodite* type features for a moment. "You have the most musical laugh...Very becoming."

She returned his gaze, and then smiled. "Why thank you, sir. That's very gallant." Silke continued to stare at his patrician face.

Riley's eyes narrowed as he observed the interchange...

§§§

CHAPTER NINETEEN

SKEANS BOARDING HOUSE

"Now quit twitchin', Jethro, I'm liable to poke you with one of these pins," said Faye as she fitted the new parlor jacket she was making for him.

He ran his hand down the front of the shiny, dark blue, brocaded, Japanese silk. "I've never had anything quite this nice, sweet Faye…Ow."

"See."

"Well, now all you need is a briar pipe."

Padrino turned his head carefully to see Bone and Loraine enter the parlor from the kitchen, each had a white ceramic mug of after dinner hot coffee.

"And a cocker spaniel to bring your slippers," added Loraine.

"Don't think I'm ready for all that...but I am liking this jacket," he replied. "Makes me feel special."

"You are special, Jethro...Now, be still," chided Faye.

Padrino chuckled. "Yessum." He glanced out of the corner of his eye at Bone and Loraine. "Any word from Silke?"

"Nothing yet...Know they got off the train at Atoka and headed toward the Shawnee Hills," said Bone as he backed up to the crackling blaze in the wide fireplace.

"My question is, who is Duce Walton working for?" asked Loraine. "Know he's not bright enough to pull all these jobs off by himself...Somebody's got to be feeding him the information."

"Putting our detective hats on, lets see if we can find out," said Bone.

"Where do we start?" she queried.

"Considering the reports have it that he was almost always well dressed...Sometimes as a business man, sometimes as a drummer...That tells me he dang sure wasn't camping out. He had a room at a boarding house or a hotel...somewhere."

"But where?" asked Loraine.

"I'd suggest we start up at Dexter," said Bodie as he came in the parlor from the foyer. "Heard ya'll talkin' 'bout him comin' down the stairs."

"Why Dexter?" asked Bone.

"It's long been a place where miscreants and outlaws on the scout go to hide...No town law. It's out of the way, but still close enough to Gainesville or Denison...an' the railroad, plus only a mile or so from the Red River and the Nations," answered Bodie. "At one time, after Lincoln's war, Bloody Bill Anderson, William Clarke Quantrill, an' the James Gang hid out there and the surrounding area of Delaware Bend."

"You don't say," commented Bone.

"Do say," replied Bodie.

"Bass told us that's where Tom Story and Bass's son, Bennie, were staying before ya'll got them," said Loraine.

"Was," replied Bodie.

"Well, what say we saddle up, take a ride up there in the morning and see what we can dig up?" suggested Bone.

"Works for me," answered Bodie.

CANEY BOGGY CREEK

Silke pulled her warhawk from her bead and quilled belt and got her small Arkansas stone from her possibles bag. She spat on it and started honing the edge of the deadly weapon.

"My, that's some tomahawk you have there, not many carry them anymore," said McPherson.

The warhawk had a three and one-half inch slightly curved cutting edge with a sharp, pointed spike on the opposite end of the blade.

"I was recently inducted into the warrior clan of the Chickasaw as a Hatchet Woman," she responded.

"Really? I wasn't aware they had women warriors," he replied.

She smiled, showing her even white teeth and nodded. "For many centuries…There are two clans for the women, the Panther Woman clan that is responsible for battlefield communications and strategy, and the Hatchet Woman clan who go into battle singing songs."

McPherson had a perplexed expression. "Singing songs?"

She nodded. "The beautiful songs would distract or throw the enemy off guard..." Silke smiled again. "...then the Hatchet Women would...take them out."

She held up her tomahawk, spun it around in her hand, tilted her head and arched her well-shaped eyebrows.

"And now you are one of them?" questioned Timothy.

She held up the Hatchet Woman talisman necklace *Anompoli Lawa* had hung around her neck after the ceremony.

He leaned forward and looked closely at the crossed warhawks fashioned of pure silver. "My goodness...Do you know how to use it?"

Silke had an slight enigmatic grin—she tilted her head forward and looked at him from under her eyebrows—no words were necessary.

"Oh." McPherson nodded.

"Hell hath no fury…" commented Riley. "An' it ain't got nothin' to do with bein' scorned."

The sun was only a pink glow on the eastern horizon as it started the daily chase of the night darkness to the west. The morning dew glistened on the short winter grass like millions upon millions of tiny diamonds.

McPherson blinked his eyes, lifted his head and sniffed the air. "Mmm, coffee," he said as he looked over at Silke by the firepit.

"Be ready in a few moments," she replied.

Riley walked back into camp with an armload of deadfall and dropped it near the fire. He looked over at McPherson crawling out of his enclosed sleeping bag.

"Huh…Never saw one of those before."

Tim pulled on his tall, black, riding boots and glanced up at the ranger. "It's patterned after the Euklisia Rug from ancient Greece, but it's made in Finland…Notice it tapers toward the bottom for better heat retention…Just have to crawl in, and then crawl out."

"I'll be darned," Boston responded.

"It's coffee," announced Silke.

McPherson strode over to the fire as he pulled on his canvas jacket against the chill of the morning and took the proffered cup from Silke.
She poured one for Riley, then for Red Wolf, and finally, one for herself.

"Got some potatoes and I noticed some wild onions down by the creek...How's about some venison hash for breakfast?" asked Silke.

"Sounds fabulous, my dear," replied McPherson.

"That's shiny," added Riley.

Red Wolf just nodded.

CHOATE HOLLER

The outlaw camp was stirring—a number of the men were sitting up in their soogans, holding their heads, hung over from the night before.

Herky had the fire stoked up and the coffee pot was nearing boil. He was slicing fat back in a skillet where it immediately began to sizzle.

The normally enticing smell of bacon frying had the opposite effect on several of the men this morning as they stumbled over to the brush and upchucked.

Duce and Merkins watched the men pay for their overindulgence last night.

"More fer me an' you, Goose," said Walton with a bit of a sneer.

"I'd say," he replied.

Mazeppa pulled out a fresh bottle from his bags. "Gonna need a little hair of the dog," he said as he removed the cork.

"Go easy on that who-hit-John," said Duce.

"Kin handle it," he replied as he took a swig.

"Who's on duty?" asked Walton.

"Damn'f I know," Mazeppa replied.

"Then get off your ass an' go find out...Now." Duce glared at the man.

"Awright, awright." He put the cork back in the bottle, got to his feet an' started counting off the men on his fingers. "Uh...Looks like Dog."

"How do you know?"

"On account he's the onl'est one not here."

"Go find out..." Duce stopped when Dog came into camp from the brush to the north, buttoning his trousers.

"Where the hell you been?" asked Walton.

"Had to drain my lizard…Why?"

"You not on guard duty?"

"Huh?"

"You heard me."

"Uh…Naw…Had the six to ten watch."

Walton glared at Mazeppa again and drew his Colt. "Damn you…Told you we need somebody on that south end 'round the clock…Oughta punch a hole in that block of wood you call a head."

He thumbed the hammer back on his pistol, but Goose grabbed his arm.

"Don't need no shootin', Duce."

"You go, then, Mazeppa. You go…Now!"

"How long?" Mazeppa asked meekly.

"Till I send somebody else out there…" Duce turned and stalked away toward the campfire built in the center of the camp, mumbling, "Damn, stupid…Surrounded by idiots…Dumb as stumps."

COOKE COUNTY, TEXAS

Bone, Loraine, and Bodie held their horses at a medium trot on a ranch road headed northeast toward Dexter.

"Glad Faye made Padrino stay so she could finish his jacket," said Loraine.

"Over his objections," commented Bone.

"I think it's sweet…. Has he ever been married or anything?" she asked.

"For a while, back when he was forty something. Pretty little thing…Betrayed him. Got herself a sugar daddy on the sly while he was on his last deployment."

"Oh, no…What did he do?"

"He let her go. Always said his philosophy was to never close a door on anyone. If she wanted greener pastures…"

"That's awful. Shows she was short on character and long on herself," said Loraine.

"It devastated him, though, but he wouldn't let anyone see it…Kind of became a hermit until he moved in with me…He deserves someone like Faye."

"I agree," she replied.

"Keeps his emotions bottled up, don't he?" questioned Bodie.

"His philosophy is once burned…twice stupid."

"Makes sense to me," replied the ranger.

They pulled rein outside the two-story ship-lap constructed Dexter Hotel, tied up, and went inside.

"How-do, folks. I'm Mervin…Need a couple of rooms, do you?" asked the balding, skinny desk clerk.

"Not today, pard, just need some information," said Bone as he pulled his Deputy Sheriff's badge from his possibles pouch and showed it.

Bodie opened his coat to show his circle and star Texas Ranger badge.

The clerk was immediately nervous. "Uh…Yeah, what do you need to know?…Sir?"

Bone took a folded wanted poster from the pouch, unfolded it and slid it across the counter. "Ever seen this fellow…Mervin?"

The smallish desk clerk glanced up at Bone, then Loraine, and finally at Bodie before he looked down at the dodger.

"Uh…Yessir, calls hisself John Smith. Been stayin' here off an' on for the last month er so…'Long with a Mister Henry Jones, but, Mister Smith called him Goose…Checked out last week.

"Goose Merkins," Loraine whispered to Bodie.

"Much obliged, Mervin. You have a good day, hear?" said Bone.

He touched the brim of his dark green John Bull hat, turned on his heel, and headed toward the door. Loraine and Bodie were on his heels.

"Best make a run by the Sugar Hill Saloon," said Bodie as they mounted up. "It's down on the main street. There are several other saloons, but the Sugar Hill is the place to start."

"Lead on, Ranger," said Bone.

Five minutes later, they reined up in front of the Sugar Hill combination saloon and mercantile, dismounted, watered their horses, and then tied them up at one of the hitching rails.

They loosened their cinches, stepped up on the boardwalk and pushed through the batwing doors.

They habitually moved to the side out of the glaring backlight from outside until their eyes adjusted to the dim light in the saloon.

"Yep, smells like every other saloon I've been in since we've been here…tobacco smoke, stale beer, urine, and vomit."

"Don't forget the reek of body odor, Pard," said Bone.

"That too," she agreed.

They moved over through the noontime crowd to the thirty-five foot bar on the left side of the room.

The middle-aged, portly bartender, in a white collarless shirt with red garters holding too-long sleeves up, greeted them. "Howdy, folks, I'm Ed Stein, owner of the Sugar Hill...What'll you have?"

Before they could respond, a large cowboy type standing at the bar in range clothes, that hadn't seen water since the last rain, noticed the badge on Bodie's vest and spoke up, "They don't need nothin', Ed...ain't drinkin' with no damn lawdogs."

Bone turned to the big man. "Were you born stupid...or do you just practice it every day?"

"Huh?" he responded.

Bone turned to Loraine. "See?"

"Time and effort will take care of ignorance, Bone...But, stupid is forever," she quipped.

The thug turned and looked down at her. "Hey, split-tail, don't need none of yer mouth, neither."

Loraine's face winced. "Ooh...I really wished you hadn't said that."

"Yeah? Why's that?"

"Because, now I'm going to have to hurt you."

§§§

CHAPTER TWENTY

CANEY BOGGY CREEK

"Well, have a good hunt, Timothy," said Silke as she snugged the cinch on her line back dun, *Lakna'*.

"Huntin' for anything in particular?" asked Riley as he swung up into his saddle.

He tied his gear on the back of his English saddle and slipped the Mauser in its boot. "I'm told there's black bear here in the Shawnee Hills," he replied.

"Be careful, one shot won't always drop a bear…What's the caliber of your rifle?" asked Silke.

"Seven by fifty seven…Five round internal magazine," McPherson replied.

Silke shook her head. "Little light for bear, I'd say."

"Range is around 500 yards. Should give me plenty of safe space."

"Except you won't get a 500 yard shot in these woods…Be lucky if you have a hundred, maybe a hundred an' fifty yards max," said Silke. "If you're workin' afoot…could come right up on one."

He flashed a grin. "Should be fine, but thanks for your concern."

"Hate to see you get in trouble, is all."

"Come by the Painted Lady when you get back from taking care of those brigands…Drinks are on the house," he said as he mounted his dapple gray Saddlebred gelding. "Any idea where they are?"

Silke pursed her full lips. "My guess is they're holed up somewhere here in the Shawnees…Red

Wolf hasn't had any trouble followin' their trail…so far."

She tightened the saddle strings around her soogan behind her cantle, mounted, grabbed the saddlehorn and shifted her weight to the right to re-center the saddle.

"Lead out, Red Wolf," she said as she turned to wave good bye to McPherson.

He touched the brim of his hat, flashed a smile at her and nudged his sixteen-hand mount into the Caney Boggy to cross it.

"How far is it to Barnett?" asked Riley as he trotted up beside Silke.

"Oh, 'bout ten miles…give or take," she replied. "Still in the creek, Red Wolf?"

His only answer was, "Unnn."

SUGAR HILL SALOON

"You know who yer a-talkin' to, woman?" said the thug.

His three running buddies stepped up behind him and started to spread out.

"Wouldn't move any further, boys, I were you," said Bone.

"Yeah, an' why's that?" asked the ruffian closest to the first man.

"Because I'll put a hole in you big enough to ride a horse through." Bone rested his hand on the grip of his 500 and smiled.

The cowboy looked at the flinty gold-flecked eyes burning a hole through him.

"We're the Fisher brothers, this here's Manny..." He nodded to the brother closest to him. "An' that's Miller an' Newt...Folks jest call me King."

"Heard tell King Fisher was killed in San Antonio in '84...for shootin' off his mouth," said Bodie.

"Yeah, well...weren't me."

"Do tell?" commented Bone.

"Do tell what?" King asked.

Bone turned to Loraine. "See, Honey, just keeps proving it...dumb as a bucket of rocks."

"Awright, that's it. I'm fixin' to pull yer head off, big man, and spit down the hole," said King.

"Don't think so," replied Bone.

"Oh, yeah?"

"Uh-huh…You won't be able to."

King got a confused expression on his face. "How's that?"

"You forgot, my little wife here said she's going to hurt you." Bone smiled.

"The hell you say." King drew back his fist to swing a haymaker at Loraine.

Her right hand shot out like a striking cottonmouth in a straight openhanded jab to the point of his chin with the heel of her hand. King's head snapped back and his teeth made an audible *clack* as they popped together. His sweat-stained hat flew backward.

Loraine reached up, grabbed a handful of his dark, greasy hair, jerked his head forward and down, where his face collided with her knee coming up.

There was a sickening sound of bone crunching as his nose splattered to the right, spraying blood over the rest of his face to go with the blood from his smashed lips.

His head snapped back again as two of his front teeth flew out back over his head where one bounced off the bar top and the other landed in the half-full spittoon on the floor. King's knees buckled and he collapsed to the sawdust covered floor in a heap like a pile of dirty laundry.

His brother, Manny, reached for the Remington on his hip, but never cleared leather as Bone's .50 cal, roared in the confines of the room, shattering the .44 caliber handgun in several pieces, with a loud clang.

The big 500 grain round took over half of Manny's hand with it.

The second Fisher brother screamed like a woman, grabbed his mangled hand, brought it up and stared at the two remaining fingers as the blood poured down his arm. He dropped to his knees beside his brother, whimpering.

Bodie addressed the remaining brothers, "Either of ya'll want any?"

Miller and Newt exchanged glances, and then looked at their brothers on the floor. They stared at the cannon still in Bone's hand and at Loraine, who was calmly standing in front of them, her arms folded across her bosom. A wry grin was on her face.

Both men slowly shook their heads.

"Didn't think so," said Bodie.

The silence in the saloon from the rest of the patrons was deafening—quiet enough to hear a mouse peeing on cotton.

The bartender had a blank look on his face and finally said in a soft voice, "Damnation…That just happened…and in less than two seconds…Good God amighty."

Bone turned to Bodie. "Seen any dodgers on this bunch come through the Ranger's office?"

Bodie shook his head. "Not that I recall."

Bone nodded. "Wannabees."

He turned to Ed. "Now, as to what we'll have. I want a Lone Star beer…Same for you, Hon?"

"Sounds good," said Loraine.

"Shot of tequila," added Bodie.

"Comin' right up…On the house." He looked at Miller and Newt. "Get your brothers and get out of my saloon."

"I'd take the both of them to the doc's, if ya'll got one." Bone glanced down at Manny, holding what was left of his hand to his chest and a still groggy King.

Miller and Newt nodded, helped their brothers to their feet and toward the batwing doors.

Ed sat the beers and tequila on the bar. "There you go, folks, anything else?"

Loraine pulled a wanted poster from her possibles pouch, unfolded it and placed it on the bar in front of Stein. "Ever seen him before?"

Ed took a short look at the sketch on the front above the notice of a $2,000 dollar reward—dead or alive, and nodded. "Uh-huh. Duce Walton. Comes in regul'r with a friend...Goose something or other."

"Ever meet with anybody else?" asked Bone.

"Now that you mention it...Yeah."

BARNETT, IT

Silke, Riley, and Red Wolf trotted into the small hamlet. Bear Dog padded alongside Silke's horse.

"Only store I know of is Lulabell's down yonder on the right," she said.

They reined up, dismounted, loosened their girths, and wrapped their reins loosely around the hitching rail.

Riley reached the white gingerbread screendoor first, opened it, and stood aside for Silke to go in.

Red Wolf followed the ranger as Bear Dog slipped through between Riley's legs, almost tripping him. He let the screendoor slam.

A calico cat on a side counter glanced up, yawned, stretched, and then laid back down.

"Come in folks, I'm Lulabell…an' don't slam that door again. You disturbed Girty's beauty rest…an' keep that…Oh, my…is that a wolf?"

"Wolf dog. Yessum." Silke looked down at the half-grown pup. "Stay away from the cat, Bear Dog."

He looked up at her, and then at Girty and cocked his head.

"He's never seen a cat before," said Silke.

The two animals stared at each other for a moment, then Girty jumped down and commenced rubbing against Bear Dog's sides, butting him under his chin, and purring. The pup licked the top of the cat's head when it came close to his face.

"Well, I never," said Lulabell.

"Yeah, who'd a thought?" commented Riley.

Silke just grinned.

"Well, what do you folks need?" asked Lulabell. "Ya'll are law, ain'tcha?"

"I'm a Pinkerton detective, this is Texas Ranger Riley Boston an' that's Chickasaw Lighthorse Red Wolf...could use a little information an' some supplies."

"Reckon I got both, less I'm slap out of one or the other," she replied.

Riley and Silke exchanged grins.

"Need some coffee, slab of fatback, canned pickled peaches, jerky, an' some cornmeal, for the supplies."

"What kind of sodypops you got?" asked Riley.

Lulabell started laying the goods on the counter. "Well, usually got root beer, but slap out of that...Do have some sarsaparilla, lemon, strawberry, an' a fair new one, cherry cream soda...Ice man come yest'day so they be real cold...In that wood cooler over yonder."

They stepped over to the square cooler made of one and a half inch thick cypress and a fitted top like a butter churn.

Silke lifted the lid by the brass handle and looked down into the bottles nestled on a pile of chipped ice—there was half of a twenty-five pound block left at one end with a iron-handled ice pick lying on top.

"That dark one the cherry cream soda?" asked Riley.

"Yep, folks seem to like it. They say it has egg whites and vanilla in it…say it's like drinkin' a dessert…cain't imagine."

Red Wolf grabbed one and wiped the moisture off with his bandanna—it had a blue Boudreaux's Cherry Creme Soda label painted on the side.

"I'll try one too. Love new things."

Red Wolf handed one to Silke, and then one to Riley. They wiped them off with their bandannas and looked at the metal top on the bottle that was crimped all around the edge.

"How do you open it?…There's no wire."

"Hand 'em here, honey," said Lulabell as she took a triangle shaped tool and popped the cap from each bottle, making a hissing sound.

Silke turned it up and took a sip. "Oh, my stars." She held it out in front of her and stared at it for a moment. "That's amazin'."

Riley grabbed his chest like he was having a heart attack and staggered a little. "I have died an' gone to heaven." He took another sip and closed his eyes.

Red Wolf's dark eyes got big as surprise registered on his brown face. "Unnn, Red Wolf have new favorite drink." He almost grinned, and then reached into the cracker barrel and got a handful of soda crackers.

"Now, 'bout that information," said Silke as she pitched a five dollar gold piece on the counter. "Keep the change…Seen a gang of men come through here in the last week?…'Bout nine of 'em?"

Lulabell snatched up the coin with a grin that showed her snuff-stained teeth. "Funny you should ask."

§§§

CHAPTER TWENTY-ONE

SANTA FE DEPOT
GAINESVILLE, TEXAS

Bone, Loraine, and Bodie took their seats in one of the passenger cars after loading their horses on the eastbound Santa Fe to Denison. Bone and Loraine sat side-by-side in a forward facing seat with Bodie sitting opposite them facing the rear of the car.

They had stowed their saddlebags and rifles in the overhead bins.

"This is a good idea, Hon, heading on up to the Nations so it won't take so long to get there when we get the word from Silke," said Bone.

"Makes sense to go on up to McAlester and wait. Red Wolf can go to the nearest telegraph station to the Shawnees to send the message," commented Bodie

"And we'll already be there," added Loraine.

The big black 4x4x2 coal-fired locomotive blew it's whistle, chugged, jerking everyone in the passenger cars. She chuffed again and after a small slip of the wheels on the steel rails, they gained purchase and slowly pulled the train out of the station.

The thirty-five mile journey to Denison would only take an hour since there were no stops. They would pickup and drop mail pouches at Whitesboro on the fly.

An hour and a half later, the trio had unloaded and reloaded their mounts on the northbound KATY to

Kansas City. It would stop at McAlester in the Choctaw Nation.

The train pulled out of the KATY depot, headed north, and in a few short moments, crossed the Red River into Indian Territory.

Bone, Loraine, and Bodie watched the bucolic countryside roll past the closed windows of their car.

The ecoregion of the Cross Timbers area ran from southeastern Kansas to Central Texas and was over fifty miles wide in places. It included ancient first growth forests of blackjack oak, white and red oak, black hickory, and pecan interspersed with a mosaic of grasslands. The prairie grasses included big bluestem, coneflowers, Indian grass, and buffalo.

The ecosystem provided for a wide range of animals, including mountain lion, black bear, coyotes, bobcats, fox, turkey, and white-tailed deer.

"This is great country for the five civilized tribes of the southeastern Amerindians transplanted to the region in 1837," said Bone as he watched outside his window, and then continued, "...in the horrendous trek known in the Cherokee language as

Nunna daul Tsuny or *The Trail Where They Cried*...The Trail of Tears."

"How long was the trail?" asked Loraine.

"Totaled over 2,000 miles and took some three months to traverse...much of it during the winter."

Loraine shook her head. "How many died on the way?"

Bone paused for a long moment before he could answer, "Over 16,000 Native Americans...mostly the old and the young." He turned to her, his eyes were filled.

"How horrible...The way we treated the Indians and drove them off their historical lands is absolutely unconscionable."

"It virtually amounts to genocide," said Bone as he ground his teeth. "It's no wonder they fought us."

"Have to agree with ya'll," commented Bodie. "My daddy told me of the way the government defeated the Comanche and forced them onto that reservation near Lawton, in Oklahoma Territory."

"Killed most all of their horses, didn't they?" asked Bone.

Bodie nodded. "Shot 'em down where they stood in the Pala Duro Canyon. Killed over a

238

thousand...shot two a minute...for eight hours. That's 125 an hour...Many of the soldiers broke down and tried to quit and were punished for it...Even harder for the men that had to hold the horses who were waiting to be killed." He looked at Loraine and Bone and his voice broke a little, "Every hear a horse cry?"

She shook her head as her eyes filled again. "Not something I want to ever hear, either."

"Killin' the buffalo is one thing, but to slaughter over a thousand horses...Well, that was the end of it...slaughtering those horses...The Comanch just lost the will to fight." Bodie took a deep breath. "Literally starved the pore devils almost to death...they couldn't hunt or hell, even defend themselves...Killed women, children, 'long with the warriors...cavalry didn't seem to care...Daddy was a hard man, he was still a Texas Ranger, but seein' all that just broke his heart." He stared out the window like Bone. "Maybe they finally recouped in ya'lls time."

Bone and Loraine looked at each other, then at him and shook their heads.

"I'm sorry to say, they still aren't much better off...Oh, some are, like the Chickasaw and most of the tribes in the Nations…Oil becomes big in our century…especially in Oklahoma…and the Indians here in the Nations start opening gambling casinos and race tracks…They've made a lot of money, but the Navajo, Sioux, Apache and numerous other tribes live in virtual poverty…many still on reservations," said a morose Loraine.

The car jerked when the engineer applied the brake as they rolled into McAlester, blowing steam from the boilers.

Loraine wiped her eyes with her bandanna, blew her nose, and put it back into her possibles pouch. She and Bone had donned their buckskins for the trip.

They got to their feet, grabbed their saddlebags and long guns from the overhead and moved toward the exit.

Once outside, they walked down to the livestock car where the railroad hostler was already placing the cleated ramp up to the door.

He stepped up the ramp, went inside and came back out with Bone's big black, seventeen hand, Friesian gelding on a lead. Bone took the rope from the young man and walked Hildebrandt over to a corral water trough and let him drink.

Loraine's copper sorrel mare, Sweet Face was next, followed by Bodie's line-back dun, Lakota Moon.

They let their mounts drink also, and then led them over to the depot and tied them to the hitching rail out front.

The three law officers tied their saddlebags behind the cantle under their bedrolls and stuck their rifles in the side scabbards.

They went inside to the restaurant similar to the Harvey House Restaurants on the Santa Fe line and took a table.

"Just as well grab a bite," said Bone. "No telling when we'll get to eat again."

Bodie grinned. "Thought you'd never bring it up...If you hadn't noticed, it's supper time."

SHAWNEE HILLS

Silke, Riley, and Red Wolf trotted almost due north on the wagon road up into the first of the hills of the small range. Bear Dog padded alongside Silke's gelding, checking for the occasional coon scat and rabbit trail.

"Well, you were right on," said Riley. "'Bout goin' where they outlaws were goin' 'stead of tryin' to track 'em."

She grinned. "Can learn of lot of things 'bout trailin' miscreants from Bass Reeves."

"I would imagine. His reputation is high even all the way down to Ranger headquarters in Austin...He's a legend."

"Them no try to hide track now," said Red Wolf as he looked down at the dusty road.

The woods were thick along both sides of the road which was rapidly becoming just a trail. The winter dead branches of the trees intertwined overhead and created a canopy.

Silke looked up. "If it were spring or summer, this would be a real spooky road...like a tunnel."

"I'd say," replied Riley.

"Red Wolf go ahead an' scout for gang...No want ride up on them. Me think may have lookout set somewhere...Red Wolf find."

"Good idea...We'll just ease along back here. Like you said, tracks are easy to follow."

Red Wolf just nodded, bumped his Appy into a trot and soon disappeared around a bend in the trail up ahead.

An hour later, the Lighthorse reappeared.

"Gang have camp four mile ahead over ridge." He turned in his saddle and pointed. "Choate Holler...Have man on lookout at south end...Got rot gut...All but two drink."

"That's good news. We'll ease on up a little closer while you ride into McAlester an' send a telegram to Bone an' them...Think it's about eight miles or so...If those yahoos are into the who-hit-John, don't figure they're goin' anyplace anytime soon...Feel better with a few more guns." She glanced at Riley.

"Always a good idea...'Specially in woods like these," he commented.

"Uhhh, me go." Red Wolf squeezed his horse into a lope, back down the trail.

"Let's see if we can find a place to set up a base camp," said Silke.

They headed off in the direction of Choate Holler at a medium trot—saw where Red Wolf had rejoined the road from a game trail to the right and followed his tracks.

Thirty minutes later, Silke and Riley came to a small branch about a mile from the holler.

"This looks good, there's some winter grass for graze...We'll wait here," said Silke as she dismounted, stripped *Lakna'* of his tack, grabbed some dry bunch grass, and rubbed him down good.

Riley did the same, and then picketed both horses where they could graze after they watered.

Bear Dog waded out belly deep in the five foot wide stream and lapped at the cool, clear water.

"Cold camp, can't afford a fire. Can hide the smoke but not the smell," said Silke.

"Thought as much. Glad we picked up some peppered jerky back a Lulabell's," responded Riley.

"Try some of those pickled peaches she had, too."

Silke dropped her saddlebags and soogan, and pulled her '94 Winchester from the boot.

She and Riley sat down on the grass, took out some jerky and a put-by mason jar of the pickled peaches.

Silke pitched a long cut of the jerky to Bear Dog, and then her strong white teeth tore off a chunk of the tough dried meat and began chewing.

SILKE JUSTICE

Riley opened the jar of peaches, jabbed one with his folding knife, held it up, and took a bite.

The forest sounds of cicadas, fussing squirrels and songbirds was abruptly silenced by the sound of rifle shot echoing through the holler.

Silke and Riley exchanged glances…

§§§

CHAPTER TWENTY-TWO

CHOATE HOLLER

A pink cloud blossomed from the side of Hank's head—he dropped to the ground like a rotten apple.

"What in hell?" exclaimed Duce as he jumped up from where he was sitting on his bedroll.

He and the others frantically looked around trying to see where the shot had come from. Duce finally spotted a rapidly disbursing, drifting cloud of white gunsmoke up near the top of the ridge above the holler, a good two hundred yards. He drew his pistol, but quickly concluded the ridge was too far for a handgun.

"Everbody take cover," he shouted. "Dirt, get up there an' find whoever in the hell that is."

"Me?"

"Did I stutter?…Move." He motioned with his pistol as he sought cover next to the trunk of a large hickory tree. "Mazeppa…who's on guard?" he yelled at the man across the small clearing also hiding under a tree.

"S'posed to be Mushy." He looked around the camp. "He ain't here in camp."

"Go check on 'im," yelled Duce.

Mazeppa stared at him a moment, and then looked up at the ridge. He turned to his brother. "Cover me, Amos," he said as he moved quick as he could through the brush and whoa vines south along the base of the slope under the ridge.

Goose sidled up to Duce. "Thought you said nobody could git over that there ridge?"

"Normal person cain't."

"You sayin' it's a haint?"

Duce glared at his partner. "No, ain't sayin' that atall…Haints is jest superstition…Don't believe in superstition…it's bad luck."

"Huh?…Then what air you sayin'?"

"Could be a Injun…mebe."

"Why would a Injun be shootin' at us?"

Duce had a confused look on his face. "Hell, how do I know?…Could be he's a bounty hunter."

"Ain't never heard of a Injun bounty hunter," said Goose.

"Lot of things you ain't never heard of, jaybird." Duce peeked out from under the tree to catch a quick glimpse up at the ridge.

SKEANS BOARDING HOUSE

Padrino sat in a dark green brocaded wingback chair in Faye's sewing room nursing a cup of her coffee while she sewed on his parlor jacket.

"I feel real bad about not going with Bone, Loraine, and Bodie." He shook his head and glanced out the second story window of the stately Queen Anne house.

Faye stopped peddling her sewing machine for a moment and looked up at the white-haired, patrician featured, retired Marine Master Gunnery Sergeant.

"Now, Jethro, you know those three can take care of themselves…Don't you think it's time you slowed down a bit?"

He grinned at the attractive widow. "Well, sweet Faye, it's like my granny used to say…Don't ever slow down, cause when you do, you start lookin' over your shoulder behind you…an' that's when somethin' might gain on you."

Faye smiled back. "I'll have to think on that one some." She started rocking her treadle again.

"I always figured that looking back was kind of like regrets."

She glanced up briefly. "How's that?"

"Only good for wallowing in."

"That I can understand…Similar to worry."

Padrino wrinkled his forehead. "Oh?"

"Think about ridin' a rockin' horse…it's something to do…but doesn't get you anywhere." She looked up again with an impish grin.

"Touché, my dear, touché."

SHAWNEE HILLS

"That dang sure wasn't a Winchester," said Riley.

"Nope...Do you think it could be Mister McPherson and that Mauser of his?...It's a smaller caliber."

"Don't see how," responded Riley. "We left him ten, twelve miles back."

"Could be it was some other hunter, then...There was only the one shot," suggested Silke.

Bear Dog had stopped chewing on the jerky held between his front paws and was looking back and forth as Silke and Riley talked.

"Think it came from over in the holler," said Riley.

Silke nodded. "Agree." She looked in his eyes. "Best we go take a look...Hate for the gang to get spooked an' move out...If it looks all right, we'll wait on Red Wolf to get back an' maybe Bone an' them will make it..."

"Yep."

"If not..."

He pulled his Colt from the holster, checked the rounds and added one to the empty chamber. Then he grabbed his .44-40, '73 Winchester, unloaded the fifteen rounds, and then loaded it back.

Silke did the same with her Smith & Wesson .50 cal she got from Bone and her .38-55, '94 Winchester. She loosened the warhawk stuck in her belt and looked back at Riley.

"Ready?"

"As I'll ever be," he responded.

Bear Dog looked up at his mistress.

"You can come, but stay close to me."

He pranced on both front feet and wiggled his rear end.

"And be quiet."

He cocked his head at her.

"Horses'll be fine, got plenty graze. They'd make too much noise if we tried to ride to the holler," said Riley.

"They would."

Silke and Riley moved out along the narrow game trail through the dense woods that led to the holler.

"Need to get me a set of those tall Apache moccasins like you and the Bones have," said Riley.

Silke nodded. "Bone learned about wearin' them in the woods from Bass Reeves...an' he got it from an Apache war chief...*Shoz-Dijiji*, the Black Bear that he met when he tracked a murderer all the way to Arizona years ago."

"Sure 'nuff makes sense."

KATY DEPOT
MCALISTER, IT

Red Wolf walked in the depot and headed to the telegraph office. He stood at the counter until the operator looked up from writing down an incoming message.

"Help ye?" said the slight built young man wearing a green transparent visor and with black sleeve protectors above his wrists.

"Uhhh, Lighthorse Red Wolf need send message over singing wire."

The agent grabbed the stub of a yellow pencil and a note pad. "Who to an' what do you want to say?"

"Want send to Deputy Bone..."

"No need, Red Wolf," came a deep voice from behind him.

He turned to see Bone, Loraine, and Texas Ranger Bodie Hickman standing behind him.

"Saw you from the restaurant when you rode up," said Bone. "Thought it would be better to wait here, than down at Denison."

"Uhhh, good. We go." He turned and headed to the door.

"Guess we'll find out what's going on when we get on the trail," commented Loraine as they followed Red Wolf out the door.

Bodie grinned. "Looks like...Hope we don't have too far to go, gonna be dark soon."

They tightened up the cinches on their horses, mounted and quickly caught up with the Lighthorse.

"Take it you found the gang," commented Bone.

"Uhhh, me find."

"Silke and Riley waitin' on us?" asked Bodie.

Red Wolf nodded. "'Bout mile from gang's camp. They in Choate Holler...Good place hide, but not from Chickasaw."

"How far?" asked Loraine.

"How far what?" replied Red Wolf.

"How far to where Silke and Riley are waiting?" "Hour…If still there…Sometime *Kowishto' Ihoo Hommá* no have patience."

"*Kowishto' Ihoo Hommá?*"

"Red Hair Woman," said Bone.

"Oh, right…her new Chickasaw name," responded Loraine.

"You mean they might go ahead without us?" Bone asked Red Wolf.

"Mebe."

Red Wolf bumped his Appy up into a smooth single foot. Bone, Loraine, and Bodie followed suit.

CHOATE HOLLER

The late afternoon sun was casting long shadows across the holler.

"Gonna be dark soon," said Goose.

"What gave you that idea?" replied Duce with a sneer.

"Well, the sun's settin' an'…Oh, yer funnin' me."

Duce glared at Goose a moment. "Yer missing a few buttons off yer shirt, ain'tcha?"

Merkins looked down at his shirt. "Naw, I ain't...Oh...there you go again."

Duce just shook his head. "You just don't know nothin' from nothin', do you?"

"'Course I do...Nothin' is nothin' an' nothin'..." He stopped and frowned as his brow wrinkled in thought.

A bullet thudded into the tree they were standing next to, plucking Goose's sweat-stained gray fedora from his head, followed a half-second later by the report of a rifle.

"Son of a..." Duce looked across the holler to the west, straight into the setting sun shading his eyes with his hand. "He's moved to the other side."

"Er they's two of 'em," commented Goose.

§§§

CHAPTER TWENTY-THREE

DENISON, TEXAS

Lizbeth's mother, Sarah Haas, sat at the small kitchen table, staring at the ten double eagles stacked in front of her. The once very attractive auburn-haired woman turned to her daughter.

"And that's all the Pinkerton woman said?"

Lizbeth nodded. "Uh-huh…Just that God would provide."

Sarah's eyes had dark circles under them, and her face was drawn. She shook her head and blew her nose on a handkerchief. "I just don't understand."

"Just told me to tell you not to worry...She was real nice...so was Bear Dog."

"Bear Dog?"

"Her puppy."

Sarah picked up the coins and held them in her hand. She took a deep breath. "Maybe your Uncle Mack will be by soon...He'll know what we should do."

"Oh, goodie, I like Unka Mack...he's sweet." She wrapped her arms around her mother's neck.

"I love you, baby."

"I love you too, Mama."

CHOATE HOLLER

The sun had completely disappeared behind the hills to the west. Day was descending rapidly into the gloaming, adding the night forest sounds of frogs in the branch to the crickets, cicadas, and birds of the day.

"That last shot was the same rifle as before," said Silke.

Riley nodded. "It was."

"It was still light enough for game, but my gut says that wasn't what it was for," added Silke.

She led the way through the woods up the side of the ridge on a narrow game trail. The trail got progressively steeper and rougher the higher they went.

They each carried their long guns in their hands.

"Only got a few minutes of light left an' the moon will only be 'bout half-full when it comes up," commented Silke.

"When's it supposed to rise?"

"'Bout an hour after twilight."

Silke and Riley approached the crest of the ridge when a third rifle shot echoed through the forest from down in the holler.

"Damn...Same rifle," said Riley.

"Shhh," Silke said as she eased up to the top and peered over. Bear Dog crawled beside her.

She couldn't see much in the fading light, just some men scurrying about down in the holler. There was no fire in the pit. Across the way on the hill on the other side, Silke could make out a rapidly disbursing cloud of gunsmoke.

Riley crawled up beside them to also take a look. "See any bodies?"

She shook her head. "Real bad light for shootin'…especially downhill…But, dang sure somebody over there after 'em."

SHAWNEE HILLS

Red Wolf led Bone, Loraine, and Bodie into Silke's campsite.

"Nobody," said Bone as he looked around.

"Uhhh, Silke go investigate shot we hear. Dark soon, be back," replied Red Wolf. "Horses picketed there." He pointed off to the side, near the stream, and then dismounted.

Bone and Loraine did the same and started stripping their tack.

They carried their saddles and soogans over to the camp and set them down.

"Looks like we have company," came a voice from the woods to the west as Silke, Riley, and Bear Dog stepped into the camp.

They looked up as the gangly pup bounded over to Loraine and immediately flopped over on his back at her feet.

"Been spying on our friends?" asked Bone.

"Uh-huh," answered Silke. "Somebody out there doesn't like them...Got a sniper peckin' away at their camp."

"That's interesting...Any idea who?" inquired Loraine.

Silke glanced at Riley. "None. We've heard three shots...All from a fairly small caliber, but powerful, rifle."

"Hit anybody?" asked Bone.

"Can't tell. Too dark when we got to the ridge up there..." She pointed over her shoulder. "...that overlooks the holler."

"No one around when Red Wolf find camp earlier. One guard at south end, but no one on ridge."

"Well, guess we'll have a cold camp," said Loraine.

"Uhhh, no need. Evil ones on other side of ridge, no see fire."

"What about the shooter?" inquired Bone.

"Him on other side. Too dark to try walk through woods."

"Well, I'll gather some deadfall, somebody can start a fire. Could use some coffee," said Bone.

An hour later, after a small meal of beans and fat back, they all sat around a hat-sized fire, working on their second cup of coffee.

Silke had brought Bone, Loraine, and Bodie up to date about their visit from McPherson on his hunting trip and with what they had learned. She also told them about meeting Lizbeth at the train yard.

"That's so sad," commented Loraine.

Silke nodded. "She broke my heart...so sweet. It was all I could do to keep from losin' it when she was puttin' paper flowers on the car where her daddy died...'cause she couldn't get real ones."

"I'm afraid I would have," replied Loraine.

"Somebody needs to pay the piper on this...causing all that heartache," added Bodie.

Bone got to his feet. "I'm going to slip over into the holler and nose around their camp...see what I can see."

"Trail there lead to south end, better than climb ridge...Them have guard there...Want Red Wolf go with you?"

Bone shook his head and his enigmatic grin spread across his face. "Not necessary, they'll never know I'm there...This is what I did in the Marine Corps in Afghanistan...Plus, got this." He pointed to the gold bracelet with the turquoise stones set all around it with the large ruby in the center that Lucy had given him.

"Oh, yeah, that thing's spooky," said Bodie.

"What do you mean?" asked Riley.

"Show him, Bone," said Silke.

The big man touched two of the bluish-green stones. The air around him shimmered briefly and he appeared to vanish.

Red Wolf shot to his feet and looked around the camp. "Whaag!...*Chukfi*...Spirit."

The air shimmered again and Bone reappeared where he had been standing before."

Red Wolf walked over and touched him. "Bone go away...Come back."

"No, Red Wolf, you just couldn't see me." He looked at Riley. "This bracelet bends the light around me so I can't be seen...Makes me invisible."

"Dang, that's handier than handles on a jug," said the ranger.

"Haven't had to use it very often, but as you say, is kind of handy." Bone checked the rounds in his 500, and then put it back in the holster. "Laterbye."

He disappeared into the darkness.

CHOATE HOLLER

"Think we should build a fire?" asked Goose from his spot under a naked cottonwood.

"No, you idiot...On second thought, lets build one an' you can sit beside it...Make a good target an' draw whoever it is out...How 'bout that?" He looked at his partner with disdain. "Did your mama have any children that lived?"

"Why shore...got a brother...Hey, you're funnin' me agin."

"What if we do build a fire an' prop ol' Hank's body up close to it. 'Nybody lookin' from up yonder..." He pointed to the western most hill.

"...won't be able to tell if'n he's alive er dead," offered Mazeppa.

"Well, now, that ain't half bad...Do it," said Duce.

"Who?" asked Mazeppa.

"You...you brought it up." Duce stared at the man.

Mazeppa grumbled and looked at his brother. "Give me a hand, Amos."

"Do I have to?"

Mazeppa glared at him.

"Awright...I'll git some wood.

"Paden, drag Hank's body over here an' prop it against that log," said Duce.

Mazeppa broke some small twigs up and made a pile with some dry grass on the cold ashes of the previous fire. He looked up at the dark hillside, quickly struck a Lucifer with his thumbnail, held it to the grass.

As soon as the flames started licking at the dry tender, he added some larger sticks and limbs, and then jumped back into the darkness.

The flames quickly caught the twigs—then the larger sticks began to burn.

Everyone stared from the darkness with apprehension at the shadowy hillside as the fire grew larger and brighter.

Bone had slipped past Mushy standing guard at the south pass and stood quietly next to a large red oak at the edge of the camp. He heard the conversation and watched the fire building with interest. A grin spread across his face.

He touched the stones on his bracelet, the air shimmered slightly again, he moved softly around to the west side of camp and ten or twelve yards up the side of the hill.

Bone drew his .50 cal., aimed at the blazing fire and squeezed the trigger. The camp was briefly lit up with the muzzle flash from the big gun, and then the campfire literally exploded with a huge shower of sparks and flaming sticks up into the air, plus a large circle around the pit.

The eight remaining outlaws screamed as one and all drew their side arms—even though they were temporarily blinded by the fiery explosion, panic fired shot after shot wildly toward the west side of camp...

§§§

CHAPTER TWENTY-FOUR

SHAWNEE HILLS

"Dang, sounds like a war over there. Only heard one shot from Bone's big gun," said Riley as he looked off into the darkness. "Think he's alright?"

Loraine smiled. "He's playing with them...His thing."

"Thing?" Riley had a perplexed look on his face.

"It's what he does," commented Silke.

"Bone's like a big cat playin' with a mouse...before he kills it," added Bodie.

"He likes to shake the bad guys up," said Loraine. "Rattle their cages, as he likes to say."

Riley looked off to the darkness again as the rising half-moon was beginning to cast soft shadows across the hills. "You say so."

"The more you're around him, the more you'll understand that his mind is put together a little different than most people...He an' Loraine have taught me almost as much as Bass Reeves about goin' after the bad guys...Just different," added Silke.

"Knew I smelt somethin' burning," came a deep voice from the shadows. "Ya'll were talking about me...Weren'tcha?" Bone strode into the firelight with a big grin across his face.

"Stirring the pot?" asked Loraine.

"Uh-huh...Just havin' a little fun...then said to myself and I knew it was me because I recognized my voice, 'Bone, time to get the hell out'...Got any coffee?"

Loraine got to her feet and filled one of their blue swirl graniteware cups and handed it to him.

He smooched her on the lips. "Thanks babe."

Fifteen minutes later, he finished telling them about his adventure over in the holler.

"Thought they were going to pee their pants when I put a round into their fire." He giggled. "Think everyone of them emptied their shooters where I had been when I fired."

"You moved then?" asked Riley.

"Yep, rule two about sniping…If you don't have a flash suppressor on your weapon…fire and move, 'specially at night."

"What's rule one?" asked Bodie.

"Hit your target."

Silke glanced at Riley. "See?"

"What's a flash suppressor?" asked Bodie.

Bone took a sip of his coffee. "It's a device attached to the muzzle of a weapon…also known as a flash eliminator, flash hider, and several other things…"

"A rose is a rose," interrupted Loraine.

"Yep, reduces the visible signature by spreading out and cooling the hot gases that exit the muzzle immediately behind the round…Not all that practical for a handgun, but is pretty essential for a rifle."

"Huh? You don't say?" said Riley.

"He just did." Bodie grinned at his friend.

Bear Dog pawed at Silke's foot and made a low fussing sound in his throat, "Wooo-wooo-wooo."

"Awright, son, just a minute." She got up, fished a piece of jerky from her saddlebags and pitched it at him.

He grabbed it in the air, trotted over near the fire, laid down and commenced chewing on the tough meat.

"How did you know what he wanted?" asked Riley.

Silke furrowed her brow. "He told me...You never had a dog?"

"Well, sure...just not one that talked to me."

"Who's got who trained?" said Bone with a grin.

The eastern horizon had just a tinge of pink as the rising sun slowly pushed the darkness to the west.

Silke was up, stoking the fire back to life and adding some larger sticks.

Bear Dog padded over with a stick in his mouth, wagging his tail. He dropped it on the ground next to Silke's foot.

"Thank you, Bear Dog." She rubbed his head.

He laid his chin on his front paws with his butt stuck up in the air, his bright blue eyes focused on her.

"I know," she replied and pitched him a piece of raw bacon she had sliced.

Loraine joined her, hugging herself against the morning chill. "I'll get some water from the branch," she said as she grabbed the pot and headed toward the stream.

"Need some more firewood?" asked Riley as he came from the woods after taking care of his morning business.

"Wouldn't hurt," Silke replied with a smile.

He looked at her sky blue eyes. "How do you look so good in the mornin'?"

"Oh, you hush. I do no such thing." She blushed and looked back down at the growing blaze in the pit.

Riley grinned and headed into the woods to gather some more deadfall or blowdown.

Loraine walked up to Silke. "Where's Red Wolf?"

"Went to check on the outlaws, I suspect…it's what he does."

"What's your plan, missy?" asked Bone.

"Well, soon as we have a bite an' a little coffee an' Red Wolf reports, I suspect we'll head on over to the holler an' take care of business."

"Works for me," replied Bone as he squatted down beside the fire, held out his big hands, rubbed them together and sniffed the aroma of the bacon sizzling in a skillet. "Yum, nothin' better than the smell of bacon and coffee in the morning."

Loraine set the full pot on a flat rock right next to the fire. Silke put two handfuls of Arbuckles in it and closed the lid.

"Be ready in a short bit. Fire's good an' hot now," she said.

"Anytime in the next five minutes is good for me," added Bone as he stood up.

"You'll get it when it's ready, big guy," replied Silke as she stirred the bacon and beans.

Bone thumped his chest with the side of his hand and made the sound of an arrow striking. "Oh, oh, heart shot." He staggered around.

"Bone…sit down," said Loraine, pointing.

He looked at his wife, grinned and sat down beside her. "Yes, dear…Probably be a good idea for everyone to check their weapons and ammo."

"Agree with that," said Bodie as he pulled his Colt Peacemaker, checked the rounds and added one to the empty chamber.

The top edge of the golden orb was sticking above the hill to the east, flooding the woods with long shadows and warming light. The trees in the Shawnee Hills were showing swelling buds for the coming spring.

"It's coffee," announced Silke. "An' breakfast. Ya'll bring your plates an' help yourselves."

Red Wolf entered camp from the game trail to the southernmost end of Choate Holler.

"Our friends still there?" asked Silke.

"Uhhh, like old squaws…all afraid of shadows. No get much sleep."

"That's a good sign," said Riley.

"Don't get overconfident, people…Leads to distraction…even a cornered rat is dangerous," added Bone. "Something seems to always happen you didn't think about…Adapt and overcome."

Bodie nodded. "Two things will happen when you corner someone or some thing…They'll run or fight."

"Let's go start the dance," said Silke.

A rifle shot echoed through the hills…

Dirt spun around and collapsed to the ground next to a juniper. A red spot was growing in the middle of his back. The shot came from the ridge side again.

The others panicked and scrambled to the other side of their cover—all but Goose. He grabbed a set of saddlebags, crawled up into the brush on the east side and started working his way north.

Red Wolf led Silke's bunch along the game trail to the south entrance. Fifty yards out from the pass, he held up his hand and looked back at Silke.

"Red Wolf take out guard," he whispered.

She nodded and hand-signaled for everyone to spread out and come into the holler from different angles. "Stay here," she said to Bear Dog.

He cocked his head, and then laid down.

The Chickasaw moved silently through the brushy terrain, circling around and up behind Mushy standing guard. He pulled his Bowie, crouched down and crept forward.

Abruptly, Mushy stood from where he was sitting on a large boulder, turned around unbuttoning his trousers to water a bush. He was face to face with Red Wolf.

The Lighthorse launched himself through the air, slamming into Mushy and driving the beefy outlaw to the ground. They rolled over several times as Red Wolf tried to bring his knife into play.

Mushy was stronger than Red Wolf, but not as quick. He shoved the Indian off of him and drew his Remington.

The Lighthorse threw his razor sharp hunting knife from his position on his knees, burying it hilt deep in Mushy's stomach. The outlaw screamed out in pain and fired his gun…

The others in the camp heard Mushy's cry and the gunshot and instantly went on a higher alert than they already were.

"Somebody's at the pass," yelled Duce.

The outlaws took cover behind anything they could find, boulders, trees, and even small depressions in the ground, trying to watch both the south entrance and the hillside.

"Give it up, Walton…Got you surrounded," yelled Bone from the edge of the clearing.

"Go to hell," he hollered back.

"Your funeral," added Silke.

"Not goin' alone," came Duce's reply as he levered a round into his Henry and fired in Silke's direction.

Mazeppa fired one barrel of the ten gauge Greener he held at Bodie. Two of the double ought pellets caught the ranger in the left shoulder, spinning him around. He dropped to the ground and fanned three shots in return.

All three rounds struck Mazeppa in the chest driving him backward and to the ground—he fired the other barrel in the air as he was falling.

The other Logan, Amos, saw Mazeppa go down. "Damn you! You kilt my brother," screamed Amos as he aimed at the ranger who was still looking at Mazeppa.

Ken Farmer

Loraine saw Bodie was unaware of the threat and triple tapped three rounds from her Kimber .45 semiautomatic at Amos—it sounded like one shot.

Two bullets impacted the man's chest and the third drilled him in the left eye, snapping his head back, blowing bits of skull and brain matter out the back—the younger Logan was dead when he hit the ground.

Walton was firing shells as fast as he could lever the rounds into the chamber.

Bone blew Paden off his feet with a chest shot from his 500 from sixty feet away.

The white gunsmoke cloud was building like a fog in the small clearing as the battle continued, making it difficult to see.

Silke had her .50 cal in her right hand and her warhawk in her left. She fired the big handgun, exploding Herky's head like a ripe cantaloupe as he raised up from behind a rock.

Duce was still focused on Silke and levered his Henry to fire again at his nemesis.

Riley saw the threat and dove in front of her as Walton squeezed the trigger…

§§§

276

CHAPTER TWENTY-FIVE

CHOATE HOLLER

Goose Merkins eased his way along the narrow game trail headed north, out of the holler. He constantly looked over his shoulder to see if anyone was following. Goose carried his Winchester in one hand and the saddlebags slung over his shoulder.

The absence of foliage allowed him to see further than if it were full spring. But, it didn't help to see the tall figure step out from behind the large white oak tree adjacent to the trail.

"Going somewhere, Goose?"

Merkins jerked to a stop, dismay showed on his face. "What are you doin' here?"

"Came to get my money…Might ask you the same question."

Both men could hear the reports of gunfire from back down in the holler.

"One would think you'd be down there…helping your friends."

"Uh…Well, looked like we was surrounded by law dogs an' couldn't see no future in it."

"Is that your future you have slung over your shoulder?"

"Uh, naw, just grabbed some supplies fer the trail, is all," he nervously replied.

"Pretty heavy supplies."

"Uh…yeah, uh, canned goods."

"Really?" The man paused and smiled. "Open it." He drew the handgun from a holster on his hip.

Goose's eyes darted from left to right, but refused to look at the man with the gun.

"Now," the man ordered.

Merkins ducked his head, slipped the heavy bags from his shoulder and set them on the ground. He looked up at the man's striking blue eyes, unbuckled one side of the bags and lifted the flap.

The one side was almost filled with gold Liberty Double Eagles.

"Now the other." He waved the pistol and cocked the hammer.

Goose unbuckled the other side and opened that flap to reveal wrapped bundles of orange bank notes.

"Hmm…Well, well, the payroll. Another five thousand…that's good."

The man reached down and picked up the bags. "About twenty pounds…maybe a little more. I make that to be about 270 Double Eagles or so…Fifty-four hundred dollars, plus the payroll…Where's the rest?"

"Uh, this was all I could carry, honest to God…Rest is back in camp with Duce."

"Why didn't he come to meet me after the holdup…like he was supposed to?"

"He, uh…just said he changed his mind. Wanted to let things…uh, cool off a bit first," Merkins stammered.

"You sure that was it? You weren't maybe going to head to Oklahoma Territory or possibly Arizona Territory?"

"He didn't say…Don't tell me everthin'."

"Thought I said not to kill anyone?"

Goose shrugged his shoulders. "Jest did what Duce said to do."

"Pity."

The man brought his gun down heavily on top of Goose's head with an audible crack. Merkin's legs turned to jelly, and he collapsed to the ground where blood rapidly pooled around his head.

The tall man holstered his gun, hooked the sling of his rifle over his left shoulder and the saddlebags over his right. He turned and headed north on the game trail.

A burst of red mist, along with his Stetson, flew from Riley's head as he dove in front of Silke. He collapsed at her feet like a rag doll.

She screamed, fell to her knees, dropped the 500 to the ground, and reached for Riley's pale face.

Silke heard Walton hiss, "Die, bitch."

She glanced up to see him raise the rifle in her direction through the thick fog of the gunsmoke.

A black blur shot through the air and grabbed his forearm in his jaws, causing his shot to burrow into the ground three feet in front of him.

Silke's only option, before he could shake the half-grown half-wolf from his arm and try again, lay in the Chickasaw warhawk in her left hand.

Her automatic reflex was to sling it sideways with a backhand motion.

The deadly tomahawk rotated three times in the air in the twenty feet that separated them, and then buried its razor sharp blade at the base of Walton's throat. A fountain of blood sprayed from his jugular vein as the one pound and four ounces of steel almost severed his neck from his body.

Duce's head flopped over at an odd angle to the back as his body dropped straight down to the dirt like a pile of wet string.

Tyler, seeing his boss go down, drew a bead on Silke only to have Loraine send four rapid rounds to the middle of his chest, blasting him backward to the ground.

Dog, the last man standing, screamed like a banshee and charged Bone, panic firing his Army Colt as he ran.

Bone calmly raised the most powerful handgun in the world to shoulder level and squeezed the trigger.

Dog's head virtually disappeared in a cloud of red and chunks of hair and bone. His body's momentum carried him forward, sliding across the ground to a stop at Bone's feet.

Silence fell heavily across the bottom as clouds of light gray gunsmoke slowly drifted off the north—it was over. There were no sounds of birds or any other wildlife—just deadly quiet.

"Riley, Riley," Silke whispered as she cradled the ranger's head in her lap.

Blood was still oozing from a deep furrow across the side of his head where the bullet had glanced off his skull, just above his ear.

Bone, Loraine, and Bodie gathered around Silke and Riley.

Bone fingered a bullet hole in the bottom of his buckskin shirt that stuck out below his gunbelt, then he looked at the one in his John Bull hat.

"Is he?…" asked Loraine.

Silke looked up at her. "He's still breathin'…but, just barely." She glanced around. "Where's Red Wolf?"

The others looked around also.

"Must be back up at the entrance where he took out the guard," said Bone.

"I heard a shot," added Bodie as he held his kerchief to the two pellet wounds in his left shoulder.

Bone turned and headed toward the south entrance. "I'll go check."

"Go with you," said Bodie.

"Let's see if we can at least get the bleeding stopped," offered Loraine.

She knelt down, took a folded handkerchief and a small vial of white powder from her parfleche.

Silke gently rotated Riley's head in her lap so the deep wound was up. Loraine sprinkled some of the powdered alum along the furrow that showed bone at the bottom, and then pressed the white cloth on top and held it.

Bear Dog laid down as close as he could next to Silke with his big blue eyes fixed firmly on his mistress.

"His color's not good," Loraine said of the unconscious man.

Silke shook her head as the tears silently flowed down her cheeks. She looked over at Loraine.

"Do you think you an' Bone can do that laying on of hands healing like he did with my little brother?"

Loraine took a deep breath and their eyes met. "I honestly don't know, honey...We can only try. Neither of us is near as good as Lucy, and she's a couple of days away.

Silke bit her lower lip and slowly nodded her head.

They looked up to see Bone carrying Red Wolf in his arms, like a child. Bodie walked along side with the Lighthorse's black tall crown hat.

Loraine could tell by the look on Bone's face the fate of Red Wolf.

"Oh, no," Silke said softly.

He laid the Chickasaw down next to Silke and Riley, looked over at her and shook his head.

"Red Wolf's gone, Silke…The guard's shot hit him right in the heart after he buried his knife in the man's belly…He gave his life for us."

"We'll take him back with us. He deserves a burial with his people," she said through her tears. "*Te Ata* said someone would die in my vision."

Silke fixed her gaze on Bone. "Do you think you can help Riley?"

Bone took a breath. "Can only try…Let's get him and Red Wolf back to our camp, next to that stream…We'll need the water…I'll carry him."

"Can you handle Red Wolf, Bodie?…How's your shoulder?"

"No problem…Had a worse place on my lip an' never quit whistlin'."

Bone grinned and nodded. "We can come back and handle things here after we take care of what's important."

The big man bent over and carefully picked up the ranger, Bodie did the same with Red Wolf. The group headed back up the game trail over the saddle in the ridge to their camp.

Silke spread a couple of blankets on the ground near the branch. Bone placed the limp form of the still unconscious Riley on top. Loraine made a pillow for his head from another blanket.

Bone looked at his wife. "You want to try it with me, hon?...You helped me that time when I took that microwave weapon to the head."

"Yeah, but you had some protection from that gold foil you had in your Stetson...I'll try."

Bone and Loraine laid down on each side of Riley. They clasped their hands over his chest, exchanged nods and closed their eyes.

In a few moments as they drifted deeper into the meditation required to transfer their life energy into Riley's body to assist it to heal—if it wasn't too late. A soft blue glow seemed to effuse from them, enveloping the entirety of the ranger's body.

The glow grew more dense and bright for a few moments before it seemed to waver or flicker slightly, and then disappeared.

Bone blinked and shook his head. His movements were weak as he tried to raise to his knees.

Bodie knelt down beside him to assist him into a sitting position as Silke handed him a full canteen from the cold, clear water stream next to them.

He took it and drained over half of it, lowered the canteen, took a breath, and then raised it to finish it off.

Loraine hadn't moved—neither had Riley.

Silke felt for his pulse and looked over at Bodie...

§§§

CHAPTER TWENTY-SIX

SHAWNEE HILLS

"Better?" asked Bodie.

Silke smiled a little and nodded. "Got a better heartbeat...Stronger."

"It's obvious he's got a concussion...possibly a cracked skull," said Bone as Bodie handed him another canteen of cool water.

Loraine moaned softly and opened her eyes. She looked at Riley, and then at Bone sitting up.

"Hey, Pard, need some water?"

She blinked several times and nodded. Bone handed her the canteen. Loraine finished off what he had left and handed it up to Bodie.

"More, please."

The color had returned to Riley's face, but he was still completely out.

Loraine sat all the way up and took several deep breaths.

Bodie came back with two full canteens from the clear branch they were next to.

"Suspect it's going to take some time and it's probably a good thing Riley is still unconscious," said Bone.

"Maybe we did some good. I feel like I've just run a marathon," commented Loraine.

"What's a marathon?" asked Bodie.

Bone glanced up at the rawboned, redheaded, ranger. "It's an athletic event in our time where the contestants run a little over twenty-six miles…Inspired by the legend of an ancient Greek messenger who ran from a place called Marathon to Athens…about twenty-five miles or so…with the news of a big Greek victory over the Persians in 490 B.C."

"Wow, that's a long way," added Silke as she poured some water from one of the canteens onto her kerchief and wiped Riley's face.

Loraine drank some more. "This energy transfer thing really whips you."

"Makes sense," said Bodie.

Bone looked at Bodie and Loraine. "Ya'll ready to go back over to the holler, make a head count, and see if the loot is there?"

"Give me a few more minutes, hon. This water thing seems to do the trick."

"That's all right, babe, whenever you're ready."

Fifteen minutes later, Bone, Loraine and Bodie were making their way back over the saddle into Choate Holler.

Bone had already popped the two double ought pellets from Bodie's shoulder and wrapped it—they weren't deep.

There were already buzzards circling overhead anticipating their coming feast.

"Glad it's still a bit early for flies," commented Loraine.

"Ain't that the truth," agreed Bodie.

They stopped at Mushy's body.

"Any idea who this yahoo is?" asked Bone.

Bodie nodded. "Yep, one Hamilton Caldwell, aka Mushy...for obvious reasons."

They looked down at a face that had apparently lost more than one disagreement.

"We going to move the bodies...bury them or anything?" asked Loraine.

Bone shook his head. "One, take too long and too much energy to bury them...Ground's too rocky, plus doesn't bother me one little bit to leave murderers out for the critters...they gotta eat, too."

Bodie nodded. "Can't argue with any of that. Figure we need to get Riley to a doc soon as we can, too."

"Agree," said Loraine.

"Let's just make a list for the Marshal's office for any rewards that are out there...Think certification by two deputy sheriffs and a Texas Ranger should suffice," said Bone as he took out the notepad he always carried and wrote down Mushy's real name. "Next."

They headed down into the bottom of the holler.

"This looks like a robber that goes by the name of Herky O'Brian...Seen paper on him," commented Bodie. "Judgin' from what I can tell of what's left of his face."

"What about this one?" Bone pointed at Dog.

Bodie shook his head. "No tellin'. That .50 cal dang sure does a number on 'em...You musta caught him right in the middle of the bridge of his nose."

They headed over to the next body. "Well, do believe this is Mister Duce Walton," said Bone as he leaned over and cocked his head to look at the outlaw's face—his head was lying at a right angle to his crumpled body...He picked up Silke's warhawk.

"Holy cow, that tomahawk makes a fearsome weapon, doesn't it?" commented Loraine.

"Yep, if you know how to use it...and I'd say Silke does...'course that's just a SWAG, you know," said Bone as he wiped a much of the blood from it as he could on Walton's shirt.

"What's a SWAG?" asked Bodie.

"Scientific Wild Ass Guess," replied Loraine. "Bone's favorite." She smiled at her husband and gave him a peck.

He shrugged and nodded.

Twenty minutes later, they had identified Mazeppa and Amos Logan, Paden Martin, Tyler Smith, Hank Murphy, and Dirt—whose real name was Murgatroyd P. Fauntleroy.

"I can see why he preferred to go by the name of Dirt," said Bone.

"I suspect that his personal hygiene had as much to do with it as anything," added Loraine.

"One missin?" commented Bodie as he added the list in Bone's notepad.

"Let's check the north end," suggested Bone. "Maybe one of them tried to cut a chodie."

"What's a 'chodie'?" asked Loraine.

"Get the hell out," Bone replied.

"Why didn't you just say that?"

"On account that it's easier just to say 'chodie'."

Loraine rolled her eyes and shook her head. "You'd think I'd have learned not to ask by now," muttered Loraine.

Bone's gold flecked light brown eyes twinkled.

"Here's the gold," yelled Bodie from over at a pile of tack and gear under a red oak tree.

Bone and Loraine walked over as Bodie was trying to count the bags of coins.

"Don't see the payroll, though," Bodie added.

Fifteen minutes later they estimated the count on the gold.

"I make it about 30,000 dollars...around 250 pounds or so," said Bone.

"Looks like someone took what they could carry and, like you said, Bone...cut a chodie," commented Bodie.

"Had to have gone north or we would have seen them," added Loraine.

"Well, let's go. Need to get a couple of the horses they got picketed up yonder." Bone nodded toward the horses in the northwest corner of the holler. "Let the rest of them loose."

"Let's check the north trail a ways an' see as we can pick up any sign first,' said Bodie.

They moved off up the trail and made about a hundred yards when they came upon a body.

"Bingo," said Bone as he knelt down, rolled the corpse over and looked up at Bodie.

The ranger nodded. "Henry 'Goose' Merkins..."

"Walton's sidekick," interrupted Loraine. "Know about him and he's wanted, isn't he?" She looked at Bodie.

"Yep, a thousand dollars on his head...'cordin' to the dodger."

Bodie did some rapid calculation on their list Bone had made as they identified the outlaws. "Make it six thousand, two-hundred and fifty dollars...all told...dead or alive."

"Good enough...Looks like our sniper headed him off and took what he was carrying," said Bone.

"About ten thousand dollars," added Loraine.

"I'd say he knew his assailant," offered Bone.

"What makes you say that?" asked Bodie.

"He was struck from the front." Bone pointed at the footprints. "See the tracks there in the trail?...They were talking and the other man hit him...I'd say with his pistol."

He squatted down and studied the prints of the other man. "He's wearing hunting boots of some kind...Interesting," said Bone.

"Let's go get those horses and load up…Still got to make travois for Riley…and for Red Wolf's body," commented Bodie.

Thirty minutes later, the trio walked into camp leading two horses with panniers carrying the remaining gold.

"How's Riley," asked Bodie as he handed the reins to one of the horses to Bone, walked over and squatted down beside his friend.

Bear Dog looked up from his spot beside the comatose ranger and then laid his head back down.

"'Bout the same," Silke answered. "Least he's not worse…The wound has scabbed over good."

"We're going to make a couple of travois." Bodie looked at Silke. "Think we can make McAlester before dark?"

She pursed her lips and nodded. "Should."

"We'll have to take it easy. Don't need to shake Riley around," said Bone.

He handed Silke her tomahawk. "Tried to clean as much blood from it as I could."

She took it from him. "I'll wash it down in the creek when I get a chance, thanks...It sure came in handy."

KATY DEPOT
MCALESTER, IT

Silke, Bone, Loraine and Bodie rode up to the train depot leading two horses with the travois and two others with the gold. Bear Dog trotted alongside.

"I'll go in an' make arrangements for transport on the next southbound," said Bodie. "An' notify the local sheriff or Lighthorse about all the bodies down in Choate Holler."

He glanced over at Riley in the travois being pulled by his gelding and led by Silke. "Looks 'bout the same."

Silke nodded. Her face was looking a little drawn and wan.

The others dismounted and led the horses over to a water trough and let them drink their fill. Bear Dog raised up on his back legs, leaned his head over and lapped up what he needed.

"I'm worn to a frazzle," commented Silke as she plopped down on a bench.

"Emotional as well as physical," added Loraine as she sat down beside her.

Silke nodded.

Bone tied the horses to a hitching rail, walked over and joined the ladies.

"Are we havin' fun yet?" he asked.

Loraine cut her eyes at him. "Not funny, Bone." She started to say something else but looked up as Bodie came out of the depot.

"Good news…"

"'Bout time," interrupted Silke.

"Southbound is due in about thirty minutes. Got us booked an' sent telegrams and the messenger over to the local sheriff's office…Be somebody meet us in Denison about the gold."

"Well, let's go down to the livestock area and turn the horses over to the hostler. We're in the first car in front of the livestock car," said Bone. "We can keep an eye on the car from there."

"Made arrangements for an Army litter so we can transfer Riley and set it across the tops of a couple rows of seats…Doc Wellman is going to meet us in Gainesville and we'll take Riley to his clinic."

"You did all the good, Bodie," commented Loraine.

"Say, isn't that Timothy McPherson going into the depot down there?" Bone pointed at the end of the building at the tall man in a tan canvas hunting jacket, wearing a gray herringbone tweed Irish Walker hat and carrying a rifle over his shoulder, entering the doorway...

§§§

EPILOGUE

A white-jacketed colored porter, carrying an olive drab litter, approached Silke, Bone, Loraine and Bodie at the livestock car. They were unhitching the travois with Riley and Red Wolf's body from the horses. Bear Dog was over at the trough getting a drink.

"Here you is, suh…Does you wants me to help carry the Lighthorse to the express car 'fore we carries the injured gentlemans to the passenger car?"

"If you don't mind. Could use the help," replied Bodie as he rubbed his sore shoulder.

"Yassuh."

The porter and Bone carried the blanket wrapped body of Red Wolf down to the express car and laid it on the floor inside.

They came back and loaded the still unconscious Riley on the litter and carried him up the four iron steps to inside the passenger car and placed the litter across the tops of two rows of seats next to the window. Silke sat down beside it while Bear Dog jumped up in the seat next to her and under Riley's litter.

Bone, Loraine, and Bodie sat across the aisleway after putting their things on the overhead shelf.

They looked up to see Timothy McPherson coming down the aisle from the front of the car.

Bear Dog raised up with a low growl.

"Well, fancy seeing you people here," he said as he put his rifle and backpack in the overhead. "Did you catch your bad men?" He looked at Riley on the litter. "Oh, did Ranger Boston get injured? I'm so sorry."

Silke nodded. "He's got a concussion and is in a coma...How was your hunting trip?"

"Excellent...excellent. Bagged a five hundred pound black bear...He's at the taxidermist in McAlester for mounting...Put him in the Painted Lady when he's done."

"Drop him with your Mauser?" asked Bone.

"Yes..." He grinned. "As Miss Justice said, one didn't do it...took two."

"Figured," said Silke.

"How far?" asked Bone.

"First shot was fifty yards. He apparently took offense to it, decided he didn't like it much and came charging down the trail to discuss it with me...Had to put another between the eyes of the big bugger at fifteen feet."

"That's gittin' purty close...What if that hadn't of done it?" asked Bodie.

"Then in all probability I wouldn't be here telling about it, Ranger." He smiled again showing his even white teeth.

"Uh-huh," commented Bone.

Four hours later, the train pulled into the KATY DEPOT in Denison, Texas.

As Silke and Loraine disembarked the car, followed by Bone and Bodie carrying the litter, they were met at on the platform by Doctor Winchester Ashalatubbi.

"*Anompoli Lawa*, didn't expect to see you here. Thought you'd be at the Gainesville station," said Silke.

"Thought it best to come to Denison to escort our warrior, *Nashoba Hommá*, home for his services. We will honor his life as a Chickasaw." He bent down and rubbed Bear Dog's head.

"I understand. Is it appropriate for me to attend?" asked Silke.

"Normally, only tribal members may be present for the full ceremony, but since you are now member of the Hatchet Woman Clan, it is acceptable."

"When will the ceremony be held?" she asked.

"It will take three days to prepare."

"I'll be there."

"How is Ranger Boston?" he asked as he looked at the still form being held by Bone and Bodie.

"He's concussed, Doc," replied Bone. "Don't know if his skull is cracked or not, but he's been out since early this morning...We're taking him to Doc Wellman's clinic...and I imagine Lucy will meet us there."

The venerable Chickasaw Shaman and physician leaned over and lifted one of Riley's eyelids and observed his eye. He nodded. "Definitely concussed...Bill Wellman is an excellent physician, we attended medical school together...Head trauma can be a tenuous thing, but maybe Lucy can speed the process up if there's not too much damage and fluid build up...I shall pray for the young man."

"Thank you so much, *Anompoli Lawa*," said Silke as the hugged him.

"I see you had to use your warhawk." He pointed to the tomahawk stuck in her belt. "There's a little dried blood."

Silke nodded. "Saved my life just as I saw in my vision."

A man in a suit accompanied by two armed guards and a porter pushing a luggage cart approached.

"Ranger Hickman, I presume?"

Bodie turned. "I am...and you are?"

"William Forrester, M-K-T Railroad at your service, sir...I understand you have a shipment of ours."

"Most of it, Mister Forrester, a little over five thousand missing of the gold coin, plus the payroll."

He grimaced and nodded. "It is what it is. Thank you for retrieving what you did."

"We're still on the trail of the rest, sir...I'm Silke Justice, Pinkerton National Detective Agency...The gang that perpetrated the robbery is wiped out, but we don't have the man that has been feedin' them the information on the shipments...yet."

"Well, I wish you success, Miss Justice...Post haste."

"This way, Mister Forrester," said Bodie after he and Bone set the litter with Riley on the platform.

He led him and his guards to the panniers in the livestock car containing the double eagles.

"Didn't seem too enthused, did he?" said Bone.

Silke shook her head. "This is the fifth straight payroll they've lost. I would imagine it's starting to hurt their bottom line some."

"You think?" commented Loraine.

Two blocks away, Timothy McPherson knocked on the front door of the small white clapboard two bedroom house.

Lizbeth opened the door. "Unka Mack!" She jumped up and threw her arms around the tall man's neck as he bent over.

"How are you Elizabeth, honey?" He set her down, stepped inside the living room of the house and leaned his rifle against the wall next to the door.

She immediately teared up. "You know about daddy?"

"I heard. I'm so sorry...baby, I really am...Where's your mother?"

"I'm right here Timothy...Lizbeth, please go to your room, your Uncle Mack an' I need to talk."

"All right, mama." She turned, entered her room and closed the door.

"Let's go to the kitchen."

As soon as they were inside the small kitchen, she spun on her heel to face him. "Damn you. Damn you to hell! No one was supposed to get hurt...much less killed," she hissed.

"I'm sorry, Sarah, I told them..."

"The hell you say." She slapped him across the face. "Charles wasn't much, but I loved him. He was my husband." Sarah slapped him again.

"Sarah, please..."

"Shut up...just shut the hell up," she screamed, and then turned around and leaned on the counter.

Tears ran down Lizbeth's face again as she listened to her mother and uncle arguing. She went over to the window and raised it, paused, and then turned back and crawled under her bed as the fight continued in the kitchen.

"You said it would only take a couple of times of me givin' you the schedules for the express shipments Charles would bring home...and we would be set for life…But, no…You got greedy…Damn you…"

She picked up a butcher knife laying on the counter, raised it over her head and stepped toward her brother.

"No, Sarah, put it down." He grabbed her wrist, stopping the downward thrust, pulled her hand down and tried to pry the knife from her.

She twisted violently around, lost her balance jerking out of his grasp, fell against the table and then to the floor. Sarah screamed.

Blood began to pool from under her body as McPherson knelt down. "Sarah?…Sarah?" He rolled her body over.

The knife was hilt deep in her chest, piercing her heart—Sarah was dead.

McPherson rose to his feet and staggered back. "Oh, God, no." He looked around the room like a cornered animal.

He rushed from the kitchen, stopped, turned to Lizbeth's room and opened the door. "Lizbeth?"

McPherson noticed the open window, the thin curtains fluttering in the breeze. "Damn," he muttered and turned to leave the room, then stopped.

He knelt down and looked under the bed. "Elizabeth, come on out, honey, come on."

She crawled out, tears were still running down her face. "What happened, Unka Mack? I heard mama scream."

"She, uh…hurt herself, honey, we have to go."

"But, where's mama?"

"Just grab some things, honey…she'll catch up with us later."

He grabbed a small carpet bag that was in a corner and put a few of her dresses and underthings from her little chifferobe. "Come on, baby."

"I need Sally." She turned and grabbed a rag doll from her bed and held it to her thin chest. Her big blue eyes looked up at her uncle.

He picked her up with his arm under her bottom while she put her right arm around his neck to hold on. Sally was in her left as they headed out the door and down the steps.

Silke, Bone, and Loraine sat in the waiting room of the depot.

"The train to Gainesville won't be leaving for over an hour. I need to go over to see Lizbeth and tell her we got the men that killed her daddy an' there'll be some reward money comin'…Have the address from the railroad office."

"Bone and I will go with you. Bodie, you mind staying with Riley?" asked Loraine.

"'Course not." He looked down at his friend on the litter. "Be right here."

Silke knocked on the door of the small house—no response. Bear Dog was at her feet, sniffing at the door.

Bone noticed the door was slightly ajar and pushed it the rest of the way open. "Hello…Anybody home?" he yelled out.

Silke stepped inside. "Lizbeth?…Hello?" She walked toward the kitchen and pushed that door open and staggered back. "Oh, Lord."

"What is it?" asked Loraine as she moved up so she could see into the kitchen. "Damn."

Bone stepped in, knelt down beside Sarah's body and felt for a pulse. There was a large pool of blood under her. He looked up at Loraine and Silke and shook his head.

Silke went into the open bedroom door and saw Bear Dog lying on the bed. "This is Lizbeth's room...You smell her, don't you, boy?"

The half-grown pup woofed.

She noticed the drawers to her chifferobe were open and most of the clothes gone.

Bone and Loraine checked the rest of the house.

Loraine picked up a slip of paper from the writing desk in the living room and handed it to Bone.

"The express car schedule for the railroad," he said as he looked it over.

"She's gone," said Silke as they met back in the living room.

Bone handed her the paper. Silke glanced at it and looked back up at the big man.

"Well, well...now it all fits."

As Sherlock Holmes said, 'The game is afoot'," commented Loraine.

Silke looked toward the door and saw McPherson's Mauser leaning against the wall.

They exchanged glances and Silke pursed her lips and nodded...

§§§§§

PREVIEW
OF THE NEXT EXCITING
NOVEL
FROM
KEN FARMER

SILKE'S QUEST

CHAPTER ONE

DENISON, TEXAS

"I forgot my rifle, honey," Timothy McPherson said to his nine year old niece, Elizabeth, as he set her down on the sidewalk. She held Sally, her rag doll, tightly to her thin chest.

The tall man with the silver temples took her hand, they turned around, and headed back toward his sister's small white clapboard house.

They were only a block away when McPherson abruptly stopped in the shadow of a large tree. He could see the Pinkerton Detective, Silke Justice, man-mountain Deputy Sheriff Darrell Bone, and his wife, Deputy Sheriff Loraine Bone, exit the front door of house and stand on the porch in the pale moonlight.

He knew they undoubtedly had found his sister and Elizabeth's mother, Sarah Haas' body where he left her on the kitchen floor in a puddle of blood—her own butcher knife embedded in her chest. They would never believe it was an accident.

"Look, Unka Mack, that's the Pinkerton lady that gave us that money…She's really nice…Oh, and Bear Dog's with her." Elizabeth looked up at her uncle with her big blue eyes. "I like her…and her puppy."

The pretty blond-haired child tugged on his hand, trying to pull him on toward the house.

He held back. "Uh…no, honey, we don't have time to go back."

"What about your rifle?"

"I'll…I'll get another, come on."

They turned around, he picked her up again and with long strides, headed toward downtown Denison.

"Apparently, not only was McPherson our sniper," said Silke, holding up the Mauser rifle he left in his sister's house. "But, it looks like he was also the mastermind behind the railroad robberies...with help from his sister."

Bear Dog's head snapped to the right as he stared down the street and whined.

"What is it, boy?" Silke looked off down the shadowy street following his gaze.

"Not to say anything about murdering his sister and kidnapping Elizabeth," said Loraine.

Silke shook her head and tightened her lips. "She is such a sweet baby." She looked at Bone and Loraine. "With God as my witness...I will find him...and it won't be pretty. He can run, but he can't hide."

"He's the worst kind of scum," said Bone. "Pretending to be a respectable businessman and owner of the Painted Lady Saloon...Wonder what kind of a trail he left behind him before he came to Gainesville?"

"Leopards don't change their spots," commented Silke...

§§§

OTHER NOVELS FROM
TIMBER CREEK PRESS
www.timbercreekpress.net

MILITARY ACTION/TECHNO
BLACK EAGLE FORCE: Eye of the Storm (Book #1)
by Buck Stienke and Ken Farmer
BLACK EAGLE FORCE: Sacred Mountain (Book #2) by Buck Stienke and Ken Farmer
RETURN of the STARFIGHTER (Book #3)
by Buck Stienke and Ken Farmer
BLACK EAGLE FORCE: BLOOD IVORY (Book #4)
by Buck Stienke and Ken Farmer with Doran Ingrham
BLACK EAGLE FORCE: FOURTH REICH (Book #5) by Buck Stienke and Ken Farmer
AURORA: INVASION (Book #6 in the BEF) by Ken Farmer & Buck Stienke
BLACK EAGLE FORCE: ISIS (Book #7) by Buck Stienke and Ken Farmer
BLOOD BROTHERS - Doran Ingrham, Buck Stienke and Ken Farmer
DARK SECRET - Doran Ingrham
NICARAGUAN HELL - Doran Ingrham
BLACKSTAR BOMBER by T.C. Miller

BLACKSTAR BAY by T.C. Miller
BLACKSTAR MOUNTAIN by T.C. Miller
BLACKSTAR ENIGMA by T.C. Miller

HISTORICAL FICTION WESTERN
THE NATIONS by Ken Farmer and Buck Stienke
HAUNTED FALLS by Ken Farmer and Buck Stienke
HELL HOLE by Ken Farmer
ACROSS the RED by Ken Farmer and Buck Stienke
BASS and the LADY by Ken Farmer and Buck Stienke
DEVIL'S CANYON by Buck Stienke
LADY LAW by Ken Farmer
BLUE WATER WOMAN by Ken Farmer
FLYNN by Ken Farmer
AURALI RED by Ken Farmer
COLDIRON by Ken Farmer
STEELDUST by Ken Farmer
BONE by Ken Farmer
BONE'S LAW by Ken Farmer
BONE & LORAINE by Ken Farmer
BONE'S GOLD by Ken Farmer
BONE'S PARADOX by Buck Stienke
BONE'S ENIGMA by Ken Farmer
SILKE JUSTICE by Ken Farmer

SY/FY
LEGEND of AURORA by Ken Farmer & Buck
Stienke
AURORA: INVASION (Book #6 in the BEF) by
Ken Farmer & Buck Stienke

HISTORICAL FICTION ROMANCE
THE TEMPLAR TRILOGY
MYSTERIOUS TEMPLAR by Adriana Girolami
THE CRIMSON AMULET by Adriana Girolami
TEMPLAR'S REDEMPTION by Adriana Girolami

Coming Soon

HISTORICAL FICTION WESTERN
NO TIME to DIE by Buck Stienke (sequel to
Devil's Canyon by Buck Stienke
SILKE'S QUEST by Ken Farmer
McGRATH by T.C. Miller

HISTORICAL FICTION ROMANCE
DAUGHTER of HADES by Adriana Girolami
ZAMINDAR and the LADY by Adriana Girolami

SY/FY
ANTAREAN DILEMMA by T.C. Miller

Thanks for reading *SILKE JUSTICE* If you enjoyed it, I would really appreciate a review on Amazon. My Author Page is:
www.amazon.com/Ken-Farmer/e/B0057OT3YI
Email - pagact@yahoo.com

Personally autographed books available at my web site:
Web page: www.KenFarmer-Author.net

TIMBER CREEK PRESS

www.ingramcontent.com/pod-product-compliance
Lightning Source LLC
Chambersburg PA
CBHW020223260626
47156CB00002B/508